Donovan Twins: Olympic Mind Games

First in the Roswell Encounters Series

Robert Ronsson

Pen Press Publishers Ltd

First published in Great Britain by
Pen Press Publishers Ltd
25 Eastern PLace
Brighton
BN2 1GJ

ISBN13: 978-1-906206-15-4

Printed and bound in the UK

A catalogue record of this book is available from
the British Library

Cover design by Jacqueline Abromeit

For Val, thanks for helping me follow my dream.

About the Author

From my early days at school, writing has been the only thing I'm good at. I remember writing a poem when I was eleven and the English teacher giving me the lowest mark because he thought I must have copied it out of a book. I hadn't.

When I grew up I spent my time being good at my job and trying to get on and earn money. I was lucky because my job took me to all five continents – I saw a lot of the world. Writing was always in the background but it was like a hobby I never had time for.

Now, thanks to the support of my wife and children, I'm able to write full-time. I'm also studying for a National Academy of Writing graduate diploma in creative writing. Maybe one day I'll have a piece of paper to prove I'm good at it.

Anyway, Olympic Mind Games is the first book I've had published and I'm very proud of it. It's the first in a series of Donovan Twins adventures called The Roswell Encounters. I hope you like this one and will want to see what the twins get up to next.

Author's note

The whole world watched the 'Acus' probe touch-down on Consobrina. The moment when the crew emerged from the spacecraft and removed their helmets had to be one of the most dramatic of all time. Never before had humans breathed alien air! The human race had crossed the invisible barrier to land on our parallel planet.

Even though Consobrina's main life form has died out, evidence of its civilisation was all around for us to see in those historic newscasts. We earthlings thrilled at each discovery. Nothing shocked us as much, though, than the revelation that a life form from Consobrina had been in contact with Earth since the middle of the 20th Century.

The record of their visits, the so-called Roswell File, remains top secret. Despite this, I have been able to uncover details of one of the most remarkable contacts between the plant people from Consobrina and mankind. It happened in 2012. It involved a boy named Jack Donovan and his twin-sister Sophie.

As adults, Jack and Sophie Donovan devised and researched their 'Theory of Multi-dimensional Space'. Top scientists scoffed at it at the time.

Thanks to the Roswell File we now know the twins were right. They were simply two-hundred years ahead of their time.

This account of what happened in 2012 is dedicated to them.

Robert Ronsson
22 April 2246

The Man with the Burnt Face

"Why can't you be more like your sister?"

If Jack had known his mum was in that sort of mood he wouldn't have come down so early.

"It's a lovely morning; you've got no school…"

Jack studied the piece of toast he was eating.

"Look at the time," Mrs Donovan said. "It's gone eleven and you're only just out of your stinking pit. Sophie's been training for three hours by now."

"She's doing what she wants to, Mum."

"Why can't you find something like that?"

"You know I hate sports."

"More's the pity!" His mum often used phrases he didn't understand.

"Do you think Sophie will make the British team, Mum?" he asked, his eyes wide with innocence. It was a device he had perfected at school.

Mrs Donovan stopped fussing round the table and sat down opposite him. "Dan thinks so." Dan was Sophie's coach. "He says if you're good enough you're old enough."

"Thirteen though, Mum. She'd be the youngest Brit ever to make the Olympics." Jack had picked that up from the Web.

"I don't know." Mrs Donovan shrugged. "They say Team GB is going to be the biggest ever because the games are in London," she said. "Sophie's times are good enough."

"When will we know?" Jack hoped his mum didn't suspect he already knew the answer.

"They're announcing the team next week," Mrs Donovan said. She frowned. "You're okay about it, Jack, aren't you?" she asked.

Jack examined his toast even more closely. She'd mention the twin thing next.

"It must be difficult being the twin of somebody who's found out what she's good at so early."

Jack took a bite and munched carefully. His mum came round the table and sat next to him. She put an arm round him. He made sure his eyes were fixed on his plate. His mum was wearing one of her scoop-necked tops. She had bought loads of them since getting her boobs done.

"Don't worry, Jack, there's something you can do well," she said. She ruffled his short hair. It stayed in place like a thick-pile carpet. "Perhaps, if you didn't spend all your time hunched over your computer, if you got out more, you'd find out what it is."

He ducked his head out from under his mum's hand. He needed to get away.

Jack didn't notice the unmade bed. Nor did he see his pyjama bottoms. They were on the floor alongside the school trousers he'd taken off a week before. Instead, his eyes went straight to the gleaming SN-ER computer his dad had bought him.

Silicon Net – the very latest technology. No chips, no hard disk. It had ten times the memory of PCs and because of Electronic Retrieval it processed data over twenty times faster. Jack had to have one as soon as it came out. Luckily his dad understood.

The room seemed to get bigger when Jack sat down in front of the computer. It had something to do with his height – he was nearly two metres tall already. He always had to show his ID to get half-fares.

He touched a button on his combi to bring the screen to life. His domain appeared and he checked the counter. "Nothing again," he said to himself.

At the top of the page, the heading 'Oooxooooo' pulsed back at him. It was his simple model of the solar system. Alien scanners, if they were out there, were bound to latch on to it. He had designed the site specifically for any distant life forms that may want to learn about Earth. He used it to explain what was happening on his planet. He was convinced they were out there, watching. But the counter told him his was still the only computer logging on to his site.

Jack's eyes were drawn to the bottom left of the screen. There was a new icon. How could he have missed it?

Somehow, someone had added an icon to his site without triggering the hit counter. That was weird. Weirder still was the icon. It was a strangely coloured man's face. It was the same man's face Jack had seen in a dream. His hair tingled on the back of his neck. It was the face of a man whose features had been burnt away.

Jack had been woken from the nightmare early that morning. In the dream he had been in a dark street under a weird, green light. The air made him feel like he was in a forest but it was actually a town. Jack was alone except for a man in a brown suit who walked toward him. The man shuffled as if he couldn't lift his feet. His face was hollow. Where the flesh should have been prominent – the forehead, the cheeks and the chin – his was sunken. He came up close, threateningly close. He was hissing like a reptile through a slit where his mouth should have been. It looked like his lips had been burnt beyond use.

Jack felt his skin crawl as he remembered it. He had felt the man's breath on him and it stank of dead meat. Jack knew the man was going to hurt him but he couldn't run away. He had to keep looking. The man put his hand out to touch Jack. That was when he woke up.

He came to sweating. He felt small and very alone. He heard someone moving about. It was Sophie, getting ready for training.

He called out, "Soph, is that you?"

She made a shushing noise on the other side of the door.

He called out more quietly this time, "Soph, what's that thing for remembering the planets?"

Sophie was heading for the bathroom. She popped her head in. Even at this time of the morning her cropped, blonde hair was tidy and her blue eyes were clear. "What? I'm late for training. This better be good," she whispered.

"I was thinking about the English assignment. What's the thing you remember the planets by, you know, the memory thing?"

She shook her head. "Are you crazy? It's six in the morning."

"Sorry, Soph, it was in my head as soon as I woke up."

"It's called a mnemonic."

"Yeah, I know that," said Jack. "But what's the one for the planets."

Sophie pulled her head out of his room. He heard the words receding down the hall. "My very easy method just speeds up naming planets."

"Thanks."

She didn't answer.

"Typical! That's nine. One too many," he said to himself.

Jack remembered how his dad had taken him outside one evening when he was about ten to look at the stars. He'd told him how Pluto had been demoted from being a planet in 2005 because it was so small. He was excited people were still looking at space anew even when he was four or five years old. It was when Jack's interest had turned to the solar system and beyond.

In his mind he dropped 'planets' from the mnemonic. It was nonsense but it worked for him.

By the time he woke up much later in the morning Jack had forgotten the man in his dream. Now he was staring at his picture in the corner of the screen. He pressed the key on his combi and moved the cursor until it hovered over the face. He tagged it.

Jack ducked instinctively as the screen burst into life. It formed into a townscape that exploded into his room. It was an animation, but he'd never seen one look so real. The roadway extended from the bottom of the screen and felt firm beneath his imaginary feet. The buildings on either side were so solid he could sense their shadows crossing behind him. He knew, if he could only unglue his eyes from the screen, he would see the strange brick buildings towering on either side. The eerie green light enveloped him.

He was still adjusting to his new surroundings when something stepped out from behind the nearest building and lifted its arm. A beam of light zapped out of it, hit the front of the screen and everything went blank. He was back in his domain. The icon seemed to be smiling at him. He looked closer. The slit mouth with no lips hadn't changed.

Jack went over what had happened. The thing that had shot him had been there for only a second but he had seen enough to know it was a classic cartoon zombie. It had ragged clothes and staring eyes. Lumps of white flesh dropped off it to reveal rotten insides. It was crude and contrasted hugely with the care which had gone into the detail of the streets and buildings around them.

"Hmmm. Zombies that get you. Let's have another look," he muttered.

He tagged the icon and was back in the same scene. This time, Jack noticed the barrel of some sort of gun was showing at the bottom of the screen. It was pointing out into the town. Jack moved to his combi but he was too slow. The zombie stepped out and blasted him again.

He was back in his domain. "Right. Some kind of shooting game." Jack's brown eyes narrowed. "Let's try again. I'll get him this time."

When the townscape next appeared, Jack's fingers were ready on the combi keys. He touched them so the gun was pointing to where the zombie would step out. When it did, Jack tagged the trigger. A ball of fire shot out and hit the zombie in the chest. It rolled around the floor dramatically before shrivelling away to a small pile of ash.

"Not very sophisticated," Jack whispered. "What next, I wonder?"

As if in answer, a new box had appeared on the screen. It had a set of arrows and two icons, one for feet and one for eyes. "OK, I can move, and I can look around." Jack was already getting bored by the simplicity of the game. Where was the challenge? As if to answer him the screen flared briefly and went blank. He shook his head. The trademark Donovan dark eyebrow, which spanned his forehead, creased in the centre. "Got from behind, eh?"

He rebooted the game. This time he was ready for the first zombie and turned his view just in time to zap the second. It struck him again, how detailed the townscape was. The view changed realistically when he looked round.

Jack knew a bit about programming. He was the only one in his year who could program text. He had modified many of his applications. He could tell the background was using up huge amounts of memory. The buildings were detailed to show every last brick. He judged the memory needed to run it was a lot more than he had on his old PC. He was wondering what new generation of computing was powerful enough to put it together, when the screen flared and he was back at the start.

It took Jack another half-hour to make progress through the town. The game seemed to be as much a test of his memory as anything else. He had to retrace his steps, zapping the zombies in the same sequence every time. If he went out of sequence or was too slow to move, a zombie would shoot him with a laser beam and he'd have to start again. Although it was much simpler than the games Jack usually played, it was strangely hypnotic. Something about the extravagance of the scenery made him continue. As he moved in the green light between the tall buildings he could make out there were mountains beyond. He wondered whether they were his destination.

After a while, Jack's concentration began to flag. His reactions were barely quick enough to kill a new zombie and turn to take out another. He'd gone further than any time before.

"How the heck do I save where I've got to?" he asked himself.

He looked round again and turned a corner. He was in a dingy street and there was a lit sign, 'Hotel'. He walked along until he came to the revolving door. He went through it almost instinctively. The realism of what greeted him was so powerful, he could almost smell the polished-wood surfaces and the vase of cut flowers on the desk.

He was in a hotel reception area. Jack could hear his own footsteps over the musak as he walked across the marble floor. He stopped and looked around. No zombies here then, he thought.

In front of him was a high-backed chair. A figure rose out of it. Jack's finger trembled over his combi. As the man turned to face him, Jack sensed he wouldn't be able to use his weapon. This wasn't a zombie. It was worse. It was the man with the burnt face. The face Jack had seen in his nightmare. The face in the icon. Jack gasped, "You!" and the screen went blank.

Hummingbird Summers

Jack didn't go back to the game. He needed to understand how the icon was put on his domain without his visitor counter moving. He texted Luke, his best mate at school. Luke texted back: *At the mall. I'll move over to the combi-point and we can hook up.*

Within a minute Luke's dark face was on the computer screen. Shoppers wandered behind him. Jack could hear the background music. It was a tune his mum trilled when she was cooking.

"All right, Jack?" Luke sat down. He reached out of sight and Jack heard a drink being dispensed.

"Yeah, good enough," answered Jack. He hurried on, "Here, Luke, have you heard anything about a game that gets dumped on people's machines?"

"What like a pandem?" said Luke. He brought a soda into view and took a sip.

"Yeah, like that but not harmful. It's appeared without me asking for it."

"What sort of file is it? Have you tried program-text?" said Luke.

"That's the weird thing," said Jack. "I can't find the program driving it. I can't chat with it. Program-text doesn't work."

"Mmm," said Luke. He took another sip. "Have you tried the Web?"

"Not yet. I thought I'd see if you've heard of anything like it."

"No, mate." There was a pause. "Have you played it? What's it like?"

"Yeah, I spent an hour or so on it. It's OK. It's a pretty simple see-and-shoot game. The scenery is really detailed. I reckon you can't play it without SN memory."

"Well you've got the only SN machine I know of," said Luke. "Maybe all you lucky bugs with SN have had it posted. It'll be a promo for something only rich kids like you can afford."

"Get off!" said Jack. He laughed to show he hadn't taken offence, even though he had picked up the edge in Luke's comment. "Maybe you're right, it's probably a promo," he said doubtfully.

"I'd try the Web, Jack." Luke stood up. "I'm off."

"OK." Jack saw Luke point his combi at the screen before it went blank.

Jack tagged the Web icon. He texted: *new game downloads* into hyper-search and looked at the first twenty responses. They were all promos. He tried: *new zombie games,* and got another list of promos. He tried again: *possible pandem + shooting game.* The result this time told him his game wasn't on a list of pandems. It looked like it was safe. But it was no comfort. He had no idea how it was on his machine. He couldn't locate the program behind the icon.

He decided to give up on it and do some work on his presentation software. He was determined to make a mark with his holiday assignments. Before long, he was deeply involved creating a new font. It looked like the text was formed by fireworks in the sky. He was deciding how many explosions to use per page when he was interrupted. It was his mum.

"Twinnies!" Mrs Donovan called from downstairs. "Switch everything off and come down. Dinner's on the table."

Jack's eyes rolled to the top of his head. He knew Sophie hated her calling them twinnies as much as he did.

They collided on the landing. Jack bounced off. Sophie was a few centimetres shorter but her swimmer's shoulders gave her more weight. Both of them were scowling. Unlike her brother's, Sophie's eyebrows were separate and arced over her eyes. These flashed palely behind the dark-black permatint on her eyelashes. Her top, trousers and pumps were all black.

The twins pounded down the stairs.

"Herd of elephants!" It was their mum again.

They slowed down for the last few stairs and turned into the dining room. Mr Donovan was carving a chicken. It was Friday evening. The twins' mum and dad had split up when they were eleven. Despite this, Mr and Mrs Donovan still liked the family to eat together on Fridays. It was the only evening when Sophie didn't train. After the meal, the twins usually went to stay with their dad until Sunday morning.

Mr Donovan waited until they were settled in their places, with full plates in front of them. "I see the world's carbon levels are still falling," he announced. He liked them to debate a serious topic over dinner.

Jack scratched his head.

"Nits on the table, Jack!" It was another of his mum's sayings.

Sophie answered, "How long's it been going on now, Dad?"

"They first noticed it a couple of years ago – 2010 wasn't it, Les?

Mrs Donovan stopped her fork halfway to her mouth. "It was after we split up. I think I remember reading about it when I was in hospital." She looked down at her chest which was showing over the neckline of her top.

The twins concentrated on the food. Mr Donovan continued, "It was probably around the same time. I remember the papers saying the build-up of greenhouse gases was slowing down. Now scientists are saying it's gone into reverse. It was down again last quarter. It looks as if we won't have global warming after all."

"I hope we don't go back to the sorts of summers we had when we were kids, Max," said Mrs Donovan. "Windy and rainy. You wouldn't believe how cold it was, Twinnies."

"Too cold for hummingbirds," said Mr Donovan. "Can you imagine; we used to have summers without hummingbirds?"

Jack was busy eating. He left Sophie to do the talking.

"I can remember them, Dad. We were in first school when the hummingbirds first came over. We did projects on them."

"That's as maybe. It's not the point. We're losing the carbon gases from the atmosphere and nobody knows why."

Jack couldn't resist joining in. "You were panicking when the greenhouse effect was making the world heat up. Now you're panicking because it's stopping. Maybe it's just the Earth getting into some sort of balance again."

Sophie chipped in, "Jack's right, Dad. I think I read somewhere about a drain hole over the North Pole where the carbon emissions are going."

"I read about it as well, Max," said Mrs Donovan. "It's where the hole in the ozone layer was. Some scientists say carbon gases are collecting there before they disappear. They're calling it a sort of carbon black hole."

Mr Donovan put down his knife and fork. "It's just a theory and it's been discredited. If the Earth really was spewing carbon gases—"

Mrs Donovan interrupted, "Please, Max! We're eating."

"Sorry. If the Earth was getting rid of the carbon gases they'd be going somewhere. There would be huge clouds of frozen gas going off into space."

"Well, whatever's happening, the improvement's not because we've been acting any better," said Mrs Donovan. "We're still building dirty factories and cutting down the rain forests."

"Exactly, Les. It should be getting worse but it's not. It's what makes it a mystery."

"Don't forget car exhausts, Dad. Especially in America." Jack sat back and waited for the reaction.

Mr Donovan responded angrily, "Them and their gas-guzzlers. They should have been banned years ago. Presidents there have always been too close to big business, and oil is the biggest business of all." An American bank had taken over the building society Mr Donovan worked for. His office had once been the headquarters. Now it was merely the UK branch. Mr Donovan's chances of becoming a director had died with the take-over.

"Well, I like the summers we have now. I know it's not correct to say so, but I don't want the climate to go back to what it was," Mrs Donovan said. "We don't need to go abroad for sunshine any more."

"Jack's right about one thing, Les," Mr Donovan replied. "We should be pleased global warming's gone into reverse. We need sea levels to go down a bit to put an end to the dreadful floods killing so many people in Asia."

"You mean we shouldn't look a gift horse in the mouth," said Mrs Donovan.

"Exactly, Les."

Mrs Donovan's comment triggered a fit of giggling from the twins. She chuckled and her chest trembled like jelly. This sparked further convulsions as Sophie and Jack struggled to control themselves.

Their mum could see they'd had enough of serious conversation. "Clean plates for the maid, Twinnies!" she said. The twins were now laughing and spluttering uncontrollably. The phrase worked every time.

After they cleared up, Mr Donovan drove Jack and Sophie over to his place. He'd bought a loft-style apartment on the other side of town after the separation. It was in an old warehouse alongside the canal. The intricate Victorian brickwork reminded Jack of the game.

The twins kept clothes and bathroom things in Mr Donovan's flat. Sophie had the spare bedroom to herself and Jack slept on a fold-down bed in the study. It was where Mr Donovan kept his computer. The three of them watched the living-room screen for a while, before Sophie announced she was going to bed. She had to be up early.

"I'm off too," said Jack taking his combi to the study. "You can have the bathroom first."

Once he was alone, Jack made sure the door was closed. He pointed his combi at the screen. His dad's machine also had Silicon Net technology. Jack's domain page flashed up. The man with the burnt face still stared out from the corner.

Jack tagged the icon. He was back in the hotel reception. He was facing the revolving doors. He looked around thinking the man might be behind him. The room was empty.

"Looks like I'm safe in the hotel," breathed Jack. He turned back to the doors and went through them. Something about the freshness of the green light told him this was a new day in Zombietown. It had become quite dark during his first session.

It wasn't long before a new zombie appeared and Jack zapped him. As with the first time, Jack was soon in a groove and made fast progress through the town. There was a pattern he was following instinctively. He seemed to know when it was important to look round and when he should move forward zapping the enemies as he went.

Then something different happened. Jack got a sense he was being watched and thought a zombie might be attacking from behind. He tagged the arrow to turn round but didn't see any threatening figures. He was about to turn back to walk further up the street, when he caught sight of a man's familiar scorched features watching from a window. Immediately Jack saw him, the man ducked out of sight so the window was empty. Was he being watched?

"What's all that about?" Jack muttered as he zapped another zombie.

The light began to fade when Jack started to feel tired. He looked around for the hotel sign. He zapped a group of three zombies and turned into a side street. Sure enough, the sign was there. He walked into the bright hotel lounge and approached the high-backed chair. The man in the brown suit stood up, faced him and then the screen died. Jack was back in his domain.

While he got ready for bed, Jack tried to figure out what was going on. His brain had instinctively picked up there was a pattern behind his movements. There was a rhythm to the way he had to move: zapping zombies, turning, making progress through the town. He was focused so much on his actions he couldn't pick up what it was. Something told him he was working with the game's program rather than merely playing it.

As Jack fell asleep, his thoughts were full of the man with the burnt face and the strange town he inhabited.

Another Day in Zombietown

Jack was barely awake when Sophie left for training. He heard Dan sounding his horn but turned over and went back to sleep. When he woke two hours later, he got out of bed, folded it away and padded into the kitchen. Mr Donovan was there wearing a T-shirt and shorts. He was perched on a stool by the breakfast bar reading a paper. Even though he wasn't standing straight, he was taller than his son.

"You were messing about late, Jack," Mr Donovan said.

"Yeah, I've got a new game."

"What kind?"

Jack poured a bowl of cereal. "Just a shooting gallery."

"It doesn't sound your style," said Mr Donovan. "Aren't you into quests and mysteries rather than war stuff?"

"It's got a special twist," said Jack. He didn't want to say more.

"Right," said Mr Donovan, "Would I like it?"

"I don't think so, Dad."

"Okey-dokey. Well, what are we going to do until Sophie gets back? Any ideas?"

Jack was on the stool opposite his dad. He had the familiar feeling he was looking into a sort of time-lapse mirror. It showed him what he would look like in thirty years time. His dad's short hair was peppered with grey. His joined eyebrows, which were greying too, were still heavy. They overpowered the rest of his features. He had his dad's looks. Both Sophie and Jack had his height.

Jack swallowed a mouthful of cereal. "We could walk along the canal to the mall. Dan could drop Soph off there. We could have a burger for lunch."

"Have you got his combi-code?"

Jack produced his combi from his pocket. "I think so." He touched a few buttons. "Yeah, I'll text Dan. We don't want to disturb Soph's training."

Jack and his dad strolled along the towpath in silence. Jack's mind was on the mysterious game. Mr Donovan seemed happy merely to walk along. A narrowboat chugged toward them disturbing a kingfisher. It flashed across the canal in a flicker of sparkling blue.

It seemed to startle Mr Donovan into talking. "Has your mum said anything about Sophie's chances of making the team?"

"She said yesterday Dan thinks she'll make it."

"She's put in the work," said Mr Donovan.

"She told me her training times have improved since the trials. She should make the freestyle relay. They might think she's too young for the individual," said Jack.

"What's it like at school?" Mr Donovan asked.

"It's OK – you saw my report." Jack remembered how his dad had reacted when he looked through the teachers' comments. Most of them had written things like, 'could do better' and, 'should apply himself more'. Combined Communications Technology was the only subject he had top marks in.

"No, I meant how is it for you, you know, being Sophie's brother?"

"It doesn't bother me," said Jack quickly.

"You don't get teased because of it?" Mr Donovan asked.

"Course not," said Jack, suddenly needing to kick a stone into the water.

"If she's in the team, we'll all go to London. You'd like that."

Jack nodded.

"Sophie'll be in Olympic Park with the rest of the team. You, your mum and me, we'll stay in a hotel. We'll do a bit of sightseeing. Make a holiday of it. It'll be good, won't it?"

"Yeah." Jack's shoes scuffed the ground. He wasn't sure it would be. If he was honest with himself it was a bit of a pain having Sophie as his sister. He had the impression some of his friends only wanted to know him to get to Sophie.

His dad put an arm round his shoulder. It made him feel under even more pressure.

"Your mum and I, we love you and Sophie the same. OK, she has this special gift for swimming. But it could as easily have been you."

Jack shook his head. "Only if we'd been identical, Dad. And everybody knows we're not identical because we're not both girls."

"Or boys," said Mr Donovan. "We knew from the start you wouldn't be identical because of the IVF thing."

The conversation was straying into an area Jack was keen to avoid. "Anyway, Dad, you don't have to worry about me," he said. "I'm not unhappy because Sophie's doing so well. I'm not unhappy at all," he added quickly.

They were now alongside the entrance to the mall and turned in. A tall fair-haired girl stood at the centre of a small group of autograph hunters outside the burger bar. Sophie was there ahead of them.

After the meal Jack decided to hang around the mall. Sophie went with her dad. She wanted to spend some time with him before her afternoon nap.

Once he was inside the brightly-lit cathedral of shops, Jack sent Luke a text to say where he was. Luke agreed to head over and Jack decided to use the time at the combi-point. He powered up his domain and saw the familiar face icon. He tagged it and was back in the Zombietown hotel.

Jack walked through the exit and on to the street. Almost immediately, a zombie strolled out from behind a car. Jack was ready for him. 'Zap! The zombie thrashed around on the floor before dissolving in a pile of dust. Jack detected a movement behind a fence and readied himself. The zombie came into view and Jack fired.

Only this time it wasn't a zombie. It was a man with a lizard-like face. He was dressed in a blue uniform. He fell in a pool of blood and the screen faded. Jack was back in the hotel lounge.

He walked out again and zapped the zombie as before. This time he allowed the lizard-man in blue to come out from behind the fence. He waved at Jack and darted behind a car. His movement flushed out a zombie further down the road. Jack turned and zapped him before he could fire.

Hmm! Goodies and baddies, thought Jack. It looks like I have to work with the men in blue.

After another few minutes, Jack was absorbed in the game again. He was in Zombietown fighting a life and death battle. He moved quickly in the strange, green light. His shadow passed across the intricate brickwork of the buildings as he followed the lizard-men in blue. They flushed out the zombies and Jack destroyed them. Occasionally the man with the burnt face appeared at a window. The game moved forward as long as Jack was not killed and he didn't zap men in blue uniforms.

Jack jumped when he felt a tap on his shoulder. He heard Luke's voice. "All right, Jack?"

Jack continued to study the screen. He needed to shut down. Almost immediately the neon sign, 'Hotel', appeared ahead of him. He hurried to the entrance and ducked inside. The game closed down.

Jack turned to face Luke. "Good enough, mate," he answered.

Luke was grinning. "Was that a new game you were playing?"

Jack shook his head. "It's the one I told you about – it appeared on my domain, out of the blue."

"So you downloaded it, right?" asked Luke.

"Not exactly," said Jack, "It's done it itself. It's on my machine, but I can't find where it's located."

"Random!" Luke was looking down at the blank screen as if it held the answer. "Did you try program-text?"

Jack shook his head. "I looked at it again. There's definitely no way into it. It doesn't have any chat ports I can recognise."

"Trouble is they disguise them as anything, these days. You know I've got 'Olympics 2012' now?"

"Yeah, you mentioned it once or twice." Luke had let all his friends know as soon as his order came through. Jack and most of the kids at school were still on the waiting list.

"You're jealous because I had the sense to register as soon as midnight struck in Tokyo. I didn't wait until morning like the rest of you poor saps!" Luke punched Jack lightly on the arm. They had a brief scuffle during which a lady slipped into Jack's seat at the combi-point. It was the last one free.

They moved away. "Anyway," Luke said, "I had a real job finding the chat points in that game. But when you're in the village there are loads of combi-points there. I clicked on one to see what it did and it turns out each combi-point is actually a chat point. Makes sense, when you think about it."

"Not that it does you any good. You can't do program-text," said Jack.

"OK. Not as well as you, maybe. But I can do enough to notch up the game if I want to."

"True," said Jack.

They were sauntering along the shop fronts not really taking in their surroundings.

"Anyway," said Luke, "Did you find anything about it on the Web?"

"Nothing. I don't think it can be a pandem or we'd have heard of it. The firewall didn't report anything. SN machines have got the best pandem protection."

"Get off!" Luke had heard enough about the wonders of Jack's machine. "Anyway, how's it playing?"

"It's nothing special. I'm zapping zombies and making sure I'm not hit. The backgrounds are amazing, though. I really feel like I'm in there."

"Yeah, good games can do that to you," said Luke.

"Yeah, but with this, it feels like it's all around me. I really get into it. It's like I know what's going to happen next. And I'll tell you what's random…"

"What's that?"

Jack stopped and turned to his friend. "You save the game by going into a hotel. But it – the hotel – only appears when I'm thinking of packing up."

"Maybe the program detects a slow down in your reaction time or something," said Luke.

"It's not just that. I was playing the game when you came along just now. I wasn't ready to stop but I needed to, to talk to you. And a second after I had the thought – you know, I need a hotel to save where I am – the sign for a hotel appeared. How weird is that?"

Luke's eyes widened. "That's not just random. That's spooky, that is."

Fame

Sophie had been training at peak level since the beginning of the year. This meant two-hour sessions in the morning and in the early evening. The nearest Olympic-sized facility was in Birmingham. It added a half-hour for each journey to and from the pool. She spent the middle of the day at home but, because her training was taking so much out of her, she slept for a couple of hours after lunch. It seemed to Jack his sister spent all her time sleeping, swimming or as a passenger in Dan's car.

Jack, on the other hand, spent most of his time in front of the computer. To his mother this was time wasted. She thought he should have been, 'out in God's good sunshine soaking up the rays'. But Jack was obsessed with the game. He was hypnotised by the way it drew him in totally. It had become his new reality.

The man with the burnt face appeared regularly now. It was as if he were watching Jack's progress. In the last session Jack had tried to zap him but his fireball was deflected by the window glass. The man didn't flinch when Jack fired. He continued to look down. His face so badly scarred he couldn't show any expression.

Jack was zapping zombies when Sophie took the call. He heard her screech. He waited for less than a second before the hotel sign appeared. He saved the game and ran across to her bedroom.

She was gabbling into her combi, "It's so exciting Mrs Babbacombe … Sue … I'm thrilled! Does Dan know? I'll call him. So when do we get together? In a letter. OK. I'll wait. Yes, Mrs Babb … Sue."

Sophie paused. Her chest was heaving as she struggled to control her breathing. She was listening intently. Then she spoke again, "I understand. I'll refer them all to you." She nodded into the combi. "Strictly no comment. I'll wait for the letter. Brilliant news! Thank you ever so much."

Sophie tagged the call off. Her face was flushed. She jumped onto the bed and started leaping around waving her arms. "I'm in! I'm in!"

She flung herself off the bed and into Jack's arms, nearly knocking him over. "I'm in, Jack! I'm in the team! I'm going to swim in the Olympics!" She was bounding around like a puppy and hugging her brother all at the same time.

"What's all the noise up there?" Mrs Donovan called up the stairs.

Sophie let go of her brother and raced to the landing. "It was Mrs Babbacombe. She's manager of the UK swimming team. I've been selected! She said to call her Sue!" She screamed, "I've done it. I'm in the team!"

Mrs Donovan rushed up the stairs. She shook her hands above her head screaming, "Brilliant! Fabulous! I knew you'd do it. A Donovan swimming in the Olympics, who'd have thought it?"

Jack watched as his mum and his sister hugged. Mrs Donovan's face was streaming tears. She caught his eye and pulled him into the huddle.

"What do you think of your sister, Jack? Isn't it just the most fantastic thing?"

"Yeah, it's really brilliant!" Jack's voice was as enthusiastic as he could make it.

"Come on, Sophie. You'd better call your dad." She led Sophie out of the room glancing back at Jack with a concerned look.

Jack tried to analyse his feelings. He was surprised at how flat he felt. His mind went back to the game. He went to his room and tagged the icon of the man with the burnt face. Soon he was lost in the hypnotic landscape. He zapped the zombies. He ran alongside the guys in blue. He saw the man with the burnt face watching from windows. Something about it all made him more certain, each time he played, that finishing the game was even more important than Sophie's news.

Jack spent most of his time in Zombietown. Mrs Donovan tried to get him out of the house but without success. She worried about how Sophie's news was affecting him.

Sophie received her official letter the day after Mrs Babbacombe's call. It told her she had been selected to represent Britain in the 2012 Olympics. She was entered in both the 100 metre freestyle and 4x100 metre freestyle relay.

The reporters started arriving before lunch. They wanted to know more about Sophie. She was the baby of the team, the youngest person ever to represent Britain in the Olympics. As she had been instructed, Sophie greeted each new arrival at the door with a bright smile accompanied by the words, "Strictly no comment." After she tired of this, Mrs Donovan took over. Each time they opened the door, they faced a line-up of photographers with their cameras at eye level.

Mrs Donovan and Sophie had to put their combis on filter so they only received calls from their contact lists. Even so, they seemed to spend the rest of the morning talking into them or standing at the door.

In desperation, Mrs Donovan called Mrs Babbacombe. They agreed the team would immediately set up a press conference for Sophie to attend. A car arrived shortly after lunch to take Mrs Donovan and Sophie to Birmingham. Jack went into the hallway to see them off.

"We'll be back for tea before Sophie goes training," said Mrs Donovan. She stood on tiptoes to kiss her son on the cheek. She nodded toward the front door. "They've started to leave. No doubt we'll see them all again at the press conference. You try to get out, Jack." She touched a hand to his face. "You look so pale. It's not good for you to sit in front of that computer all day."

"I'm fine, Mum, honest," said Jack. He turned to Sophie and smiled and patted her on the shoulder. "Good luck, Sis," he said.

"I'm so nervous," she answered making the goofy smiling face he remembered from years before.

"You'll be fine," he said. "Don't let them get to you. Just concentrate on your swimming." He realised he was sounding like their father. He grinned at her. "I'll talk to the guys outside and make a deal to sell pictures of you and me when we were kids. I'm sure they'll pay zillions for the bath-time ones!"

She punched him on the arm so hard it hurt. "You dare!"

Mrs Donovan opened the front door and ushered Sophie down the garden path to the black limousine. Jack could hear her saying, "Strictly no comment", to the few reporters who remained. Someone called to them to stop by the car and they stood together, Sophie a head taller than her mother, while the photographers did their work. Then they were in the car and away. Jack closed the door and turned back into the empty house.

He returned to the strange town with the green light. He left the hotel and walked alongside the parked cars beneath the towering brick walls. He was getting nearer to the mountain he could see beyond the buildings but it was slow progress.

Every so often a zombie, his flesh dripping like a burning candle, would jump into view and Jack would zap him. His instinct had become so well-tuned he was now always quicker than the zombies. One of the lizard-men in blue would walk out of a doorway occasionally and, again, Jack would almost know he was there before it happened. So Jack would hold his fire until the guy in blue chased a couple of zombies out of hiding and Jack would zap them as well.

Jack caught sight of the man with the featureless face watching from windows. He could tell the man was waiting – but waiting for what?

At three o'clock, Jack's combi alarm beeped. He had set it so as not to miss the live broadcast. His mind was dragged out of Zombietown. He looked round for a hotel entrance and there was one at the next corner. He went to it and walked in. The screen faded.

He re-tuned his combi and the screen jumped into life again. An announcer was saying they were going live to the swimming team press conference. The picture changed and they were in a conference room. The camera looked out over an audience toward a stage. Jack could see a table with a cluster of microphones standing on it.

A black woman walked on to the stage and sat down. She was wearing a blue blazer over a white dress. A white straw hat was perched on her head and it had red, white and blue bands. She tapped one of the microphones, which screeched in response. She coughed and perched a pair of glasses on her nose. They had half-size lenses she peered over when she looked up at the camera.

She took out a piece of paper and started reading aloud, "My name is Sue Babbacombe. I am the manager of the 2012 Olympics British swim team. We announced our team earlier today, as you know." She looked up over her glasses as if waiting for a reaction. When none came she continued, "We announced the selection of Sophie Donovan in the 100 metre freestyle events and, as you know," she looked up again, "As you know, Sophie is thirteen years old. This makes her the youngest-ever competitor to be selected for the British team in the Olympics. Understandably," she looked up again. Jack could sense the men and women in the audience were getting impatient. "Understandably, this has created a lot of interest in the media and we have called this press conference so you can meet Sophie and get to know a little bit about her. We hope that, after this, you will allow Sophie to resume her normal life without interference."

Mrs Babbacombe looked up again. She seemed to be waiting for the people in the room to agree to what she was asking, but there was no response.

She spoke again, "We will meet the media next at the official team press call in a week's time. This hastily arranged conference is to introduce Sophie, so without further ado, I'm very pleased to introduce you to Sophie Donovan."

Mrs Babbacombe looked to one side and Sophie was there on stage taking her seat behind the microphones. She had changed her outfit since she said goodbye to Jack. She had switched her usual black look for the official white 'Team GB' T-shirt with red and blue trimmings and blue tracksuit bottoms. He thought her hair looked blonder on screen and put this down to the lights. He recognised her nervous smile that showed off her teeth. There was a pause, while the cameras clicked and whirred.

Sophie took out a piece of paper and started reading slowly, "It is big honour for me to have been chosen to represent my country. I was only six years old when it was announced that this year's Olympics would be in London. I had been a member of my local swimming club for three years. I was racing against – and losing to – girls who were twice my age. It was my coach, Dan Mason, who spotted my potential. He has owned up since that he was always aiming for these Games. He only shared the dream with me and my family two years ago when I became U16 national champion.

"Dan tells me I should go into every race expecting to win but I have to be realistic. I regard the 2016 games as my real goal. I'm very grateful to the team management for giving me this opportunity to get the Olympic experience this time round. It will help me a lot. As far as these games are concerned I know how my personal best time stacks up against the best swimmers in the world. I think I'll do well to reach the quarter-finals. I know Dan will demand more." Sophie smiled and looked to one side where, Jack assumed, Dan stood in the wings.

"As for the relay," she continued, "I hope I can earn my place in the team through some good performances in the heats. It would be amazing if I can help us win a medal." Sophie turned to the team manager and then continued to read from her script. "Mrs Babbacombe has put together some details about me on the paper that will be distributed afterwards. Now I am prepared to answer a few questions about my swimming."

Mrs Babbacombe leant across and grabbed one of the microphones. She looked for a second as if she would slip below the table if she let go. "Please respect Sophie's age and restrict your questions to the subject of her swimming."

One of the seated figures in front of the camera raised a pen and Mrs Babbacombe pointed to him. "How much training do you do, Sophie?" he asked, in an accent half-way between English and Australian.

"About four hours a day," she answered. Somebody in the room whistled. Sophie ignored him and said, "That includes gym work. The details of my training schedule are on the sheet."

Mrs Babbacombe pointed again.

"It doesn't leave much time for schoolwork. How do you cope?"

Sophie smiled. "I sometimes miss assignment deadlines but I do my best to keep up. The teachers at school are very understanding."

"I bet you win the school lots of trophies at swim meets!" This was from a woman with an American accent. Sophie smiled. Jack recalled how his sister had won loads of different events in her age group at the district and regional competitions and at various distances. Her medal haul was only limited when the events were scheduled one after the other. Even Sophie needed recovery time.

A distinctive cockney voice was heard. "It doesn't sound like you have time for boyfriends, Sophie. Any boys on the scene?"

Mrs Babbacombe spoke before Sophie could answer. "Trust the *Sun* to have a short attention span, Dave. It's questions on swimming only, remember?"

The cockney voice responded, "You're right, Sue, sorry. OK, Sophie, do you like swimming when you go on holiday?"

The edges of Sophie's mouth turned down and she frowned, "Yeah, I like swimming any time. In the pool, in the sea. Makes no difference."

The man from the *Sun* came back before anybody else could get in. "And do you wear a bikini?"

The rest of the journalists in the room groaned. Sophie looked puzzled and Mrs Babbacombe intervened, "OK you had your chance. No more questions and if you don't like it, you know who to blame." She shot a look at the man she had called Dave. "Now it's up to you to keep your side of the bargain. Please don't harass Sophie or any of my team until the photo-call next week."

The screen picture switched back to the studio where a presenter said, "That's all from the press conference. We have seen the details sheet that was handed out and can confirm Sophie Donovan will be the youngest competitor, to represent Britain at the Olympics. She is 36 days younger than Sharron Davies who, also at thirteen, swam in the Montreal Olympics in 1976. Sophie lives and trains in the Midlands. Her father works for an international bank and her mother looks after the home. Sophie has a twin brother, Jack, who attends the same school. She has won swimming medals at…"

Jack sighed and switched the combi back to his computer. His domain came up. The visitor count still only registered his own activity. There were no others. His eyes were drawn to the icon and he tagged it. In less than a minute he was lost in the game.

Game Over

Mrs Donovan insisted Jack came down to watch the news that evening. Dan had taken Sophie to training, leaving Jack and his mum alone. They sat in front of the living-room screen and Mrs Donovan sat up straight when the presenter introduced the part about Sophie's selection. "Look there's our house!" she exclaimed, as if Jack hadn't recognised the white walls, white-framed windows and sturdy wood-stained front door. "Oh! The shame – look at my hair!" she squealed as the camera followed her and Sophie down the garden path.

Jack decided not to comment about the way his mum pushed her chest out as she and Sophie stood by the black car.

Then the picture cut away to the press conference and showed an edited version of Sophie's statement. They didn't show the follow-up questions.

Mrs Donovan sat back in the deep-cushioned sofa. "How about that, then? Your sister's the star of the team and the Olympics haven't even started yet. Still she's worked hard for it." She looked at Jack and her head shook slightly. He steeled himself for what she would say next.

"I was going to save this as a surprise on Friday, Jack, but I'll tell you now. Your dad and I reserved two rooms in a four-star hotel in London ages ago on the chance Sophie would make it. You can't get a room for love nor money now. I called them this morning after we heard the news. It's all confirmed. Dad's taken the time off work. We'll be there in London for Sophie's events. Staying at a swanky hotel!"

"Two rooms, how will that work out?" Jack asked. His eyes were fixed on a spot on the carpet.

"They're twin rooms – single beds. You'll be sharing with your dad and I'll be on my own," said Mrs Donovan.

"Oh! Yeah, of course," said Jack.

"Well! You could sound a bit more enthusiastic," Mrs Donovan said.

"Yeah. Sorry. It's just, I was a bit confused. Yeah! It's great! London – which hotel?"

"It's near Covent Garden – it's quite lively round there. It'll be fun – eating out every night. Going to the new Aquatic Centre for Sophie's events."

Jack thought about it while his mum turned back to the screen. It would be an adventure. Nobody else in his class was going. He'd only been to London once before. It was when his mum and dad were together. They'd stayed in a family room in a cheap hotel on the outskirts. He preferred the idea of a flash hotel in the middle. He would make sure to order something on room service.

Sophie's selection was on the front pages of three of the armful of newspapers Mrs Donovan brought into the house next morning. They all carried a picture of Sophie standing next to Sue Babbacombe at the press conference. Jack watched as Mrs Donovan scanned the rest of the papers. He knew what she was looking for. At last, she closed the final one and said in a flat voice, "Thank goodness for that. No pictures of me with Sophie. My hair was such a mess!"

She turned back to the paper with the longest article. After reading it for a few seconds she said, "Listen to this, Jack, *Sophie has a twin brother, Jack, who goes to the same school.* You get a mention too!"

Jack couldn't wait to finish his breakfast and go upstairs.

It was as if his room was a doorway to Zombietown. He was compelled to tag the icon as soon as he sat down. He began roaming the streets. The brick walls shone in the green-tinged light. The zombies were now so predictable Jack was muttering to them to show themselves before he

31

knew they were there. "Come out you, behind the fence," he'd say, and the zombie would appear so Jack could zap him. "Where are you, bluey?" he'd ask in anticipation of one of the lizard-men coming into view.

"Zap! Zap! Zap! Three more dead," Jack muttered. In any other game, he would find this predictability boring but something kept him playing. He didn't feel the need to find a chat point so he could notch up the difficulty.

The one thing Jack couldn't anticipate was when the man with the burnt face would appear. He was random. Every so often he would appear at a window, watching Jack's progress, but he would always disappear before Jack could take any action against him.

Then it happened. Jack had turned down a new street. The traffic was dense with lots of parked cars. He could see the mountain peaks, closer now than they were when he started the game. He did a rough calculation. It must have been over twenty hours playing time ago.

One of the cars slowed as it passed. Jack got ready to zap the zombies travelling in it. He couldn't see who was in the car. The windows were blacked out.

It stopped further up the street. That hadn't happened before. The cars usually carried on past. The door opened and Jack prepared to fire. Something told him, though, that it wasn't going to be a zombie and it wasn't going to be a lizard-man in blue.

The trouser legs of a brown suit appeared first. Then the rest of the body came into view. The man wore a brown jacket. Finally the head showed. It was the man with the burnt face; the man from Jack's dream. He was standing looking at Jack, his arms held wide from his sides. He was showing Jack he had no weapon.

The man took a step toward him. Jack began sweating. It was so real. It was as real as the dream that had started it all. Jack felt the need to back away. He tagged the direction key, nothing. He tried to turn to one side, nothing. He was gripped in place by the presence of the man in the brown suit.

Jack had an idea. "Hotel!" he said. "Come on give me a hotel. I need to save the game!" Nothing happened.

In desperation, Jack did the only thing left. He tagged the 'off' button on his combi. Zombietown stayed on the screen. The man with the burnt face was still there. He took another step toward him.

Jack looked at the man's face. He was trying to see whether he was friendly. But the man's features no longer existed. His skin was raw. His eyes were half-hidden behind thick, scaly eyelids. He had no eyebrows. His nose was just a stub. His lips were dry, frayed edges to what was left of his mouth. His skin looked as thin as tissue paper. There was nothing to betray what he was thinking.

Jack tagged the 'off' button again. Once. Twice. Nothing.

He had only one thing left. He raised the barrel of his gun. The man stopped. Jack made sure the cross-hairs were over the man's chest. The man stood still. His arms moved further away from his body. He was inviting Jack to shoot. Jack tagged the trigger.

The ball of fire hit the man full in the chest. He rocked back for a second and then exploded. His body disintegrated into millions of bright particles that flashed to the edges of the screen. It was as if Jack had set off a gigantic firework that lit up the whole of Zombietown.

The background changed. The light was different. It was a more familiar bluish colour. The buildings were gone. Jack was now in the country. He was standing by the sea. Low waves tumbled in. Tree-covered hills loomed up alongside the shoreline to one side. The ground beneath him was sandy with patches of grass growing.

As Jack stood there, the firework particles which had disappeared now zoomed back into view. They reversed their previous path. The flash was as bright as before but now the lights were coming together. They formed the figure of a man. It was the man with the burnt face again. He turned away from Jack and walked into the sea. He was still dressed in the suit. The low-breaking waves swirled around his knees. He stopped and peeled off his gloves very deliberately. Then he walked a few metres further, beyond where the waves turned in on themselves. The water was still shallow. He carried on until his hands, which hung loosely at his sides, were immersed. Then, and only then, did the computer finally respond to Jack's request to close down and the screen went blank.

Jack was trembling. His skin seemed to be crawling with biting insects. His blood was solid in his veins. He shrugged his shoulders to get it moving again. His brain was racing. What have I done? What did it mean? But no answers came.

He turned the computer on. He had to wiggle his fingers to make them respond properly. The domain page flashed up as usual. The icon of the man with the burnt face had gone. He couldn't access the game. His visitor log had clicked forward one number to register his own visit but no one else had been there.

Jack was lost without the game. He needed to talk to somebody. He called up Luke but there was no response. He left a text.

His sister had come home from training while he was in his room and he found her sun-bathing in the garden. He joined her under the UV screen. She was wearing one of her competition swimsuits.

"Hey, Soph. What you doing?" he asked as he sat down and took off his T-shirt.

"What's it look like?"

"OK. OK." Jack held his hands up. "What's rattling you?"

She sighed. "It's all this fuss – seeing it on screen and in the papers. It's brought home what it actually means." She pushed her shades to the top of head as she turned to face him. "There'll be millions watching me. It makes my knees knock just to think about it."

"You'll be fine, Sis," he said. "You'll be totally focused on the competition once you get in the village. You'll forget what's happening outside. That's one of the things we both have. We give all our attention to what we're doing."

"And what's that in your case, Jack? Hanging round the mall with Luke?" She smiled to take the sting out of the words.

"Good one!" said Jack. "Actually, there has been something I've been working on lately—"

Sophie interrupted, "Secretly, all alone in your room, for hours on end."

"Cut it out, Sis. I think this is serious. Not as important as the Olympics, maybe, but it's got me rattled."

"Sorry, Jack. Tell your Sis what it's all about." She sank back on the lounger and flipped her glasses back over her eyes. Jack noticed the sun was bringing out the freckles on her nose and across her cheek bones.

Jack wasn't sure he wanted to share the game with her. While he pondered what to say, he watched a red-throated hummingbird hover at the feeder.

"Before I do, Soph, can you answer a question?"

"Go on," she drawled sleepily.

"You're sunbathing, right?"

Sophie nodded.

"Why are you wearing that cossie then and not a bikini?"

"Good question!" Jack had touched a raw nerve. "Mum says I should get some colour in my skin before I go on television again. So she sent me upstairs to change. I come down in my bikini. Right? "Oh no!" says Mum. "You can't wear that in the garden. What if there any photographers about?" So I have to go back upstairs and get this cover-up cossie on. I only hope the pattern matches the team cossie or I'm going to have pale edges on screen."

"You can always wear make-up." Jack thought he was joking.

She sneered, "Not possible. Some of the girls do but it'd slow me up."

Jack couldn't tell whether Sophie was joking as well. He decided to talk about what was troubling him. "I've been playing this computer game, Sophie."

"So what's new?"

"Quite a lot, actually. For a start, it appeared on my computer without me asking to download it or anything. It got on my domain without whoever put it there triggering my visitor counter."

"What does it mean?" asked Sophie.

"It means it's a mystery. You can't do that. You can't mess about with somebody's domain without visiting it. When you log on you get counted."

"Maybe the counter's not working."

"It always records my visits."

"So the person who put it there stopped the visit counter working. Doesn't seem to be special to me."

"But, why go to that trouble?" asked Jack.

"Did it make you more curious about what they put on there? Did it make you keener to play the game?"

Jack thought about it. "Yeah. I suppose it did." Jack went on to tell his sister all about the game. He described the strange green-lit townscape, the zombies he killed, the lizard-men and finally the man with the burnt face. "He was scary. I seem to have the order of how things happened mixed up. But I'm sure I saw his face in a nightmare even before the game arrived."

"I have to say the game sounds pretty boring to me, Jack." Sophie's voice was slow and her eyes were drooping. She was nearly asleep.

"The game itself was boring, Soph, you're right. But while I was playing, it wasn't about the game. It was if the game was a way of doing something else. It was like an elaborate code. I got the feeling that doing everything in the right order for hours on end was leading to something."

"And did it?"

"I don't know. At the end the man with the burnt face came toward me and I had no alternative but to zap him as well. It was like the dream. I had to stop him from touching me." Jack felt waves of cold perspiration break out on his upper body as he recalled that moment.

"And did you?"

"Yes, I zapped him and he sort of exploded."

"That was it?"

"It was like setting off one of those fireworks that explode in the sky. All the bits of him were like points of light blasting across the screen. Then when the screen came back to normal the scenery was different and the explosion was sort of reversed. The man stood in front of me again."

"Did you zap him again?"

"No. My gun wasn't there any more. Besides, this time he turned away and walked into the water."

"What water?"

"In the new scene we were next to the sea," Jack answered absent-mindedly. Talking to Sophie had helped him arrange his own thoughts and an incredible idea was forming in his mind.

"What happened next?" Sophie asked.

"The screen went blank and the game was over. I went back to restart it but the icon had disappeared."

"It sounds crazy," said Sophie. "But, with everybody having access to machines through combi-points, there are bound to be lots more of these rogue programs around. What do you call them, pandems?"

"Pandems," agreed Jack. His mind was still working on what was behind the game. "I checked the Web. Luke has as well. It's not a pandem or a promo."

"What's a promo?"

"A come-on to buy a product, like on the screen." Jack sensed his sister was drifting away. He tried to put together the thoughts that had come to him while he was describing the game.

What if it wasn't merely a game? he asked himself. What if he was right and playing it was building something in his computer? What if the thing he was building was another computer program, one that had another purpose?

The questions tumbled over each other. What if shooting the man with the burnt face had actually executed the program? Did the man somehow explode and come back together again? Did he get exploded in Zombietown? Was he re-formed by the sea? Where was it?

His thoughts raced on. Who would have the technology to steal into his computer and put the program in there? Jack thought about the morning he'd asked Sophie about the mnemonic. It had been before the game arrived. He had dreamt about the man with the burnt face first. Could his dreams have been guided by something external? Was it the same superior intelligence that had tampered with his domain without leaving a trace?"

The answers to these questions led Jack to one conclusion. Someone or something very clever indeed had visited his web domain. The greater intelligence, whatever it was, had led him into playing the game and it had completed something on his computer that was important to them. His blood ran like ice in his veins. What had he done?

The next question was so awful his brain spun to even contemplate it. Who had he done it for? He could hardly dare conceive the answer, it was so dreadful. He could not escape the awful conclusion his domain page had worked as he had intended. He had been visited by aliens.

Amnugen Corporation

The rest of the week went by uneventfully. The family ate together on the Friday following Sophie's selection and celebrated her achievement. The twins were allowed to have a half-glass of sparkling wine before dinner. They stayed with Mr Donovan for the weekend and had some screen-time together when Sophie wasn't training. Jack hung around the mall with Luke and they met up with some other friends but it all seemed pointless to Jack. He didn't have the game. Nor had the aliens, and he was convinced it was aliens, contacted him again. He had put some new content on his domain to show he knew they had visited. But there had been no response.

He realised how obsessed he had been by it because it now left such a gap in his life. His mind kept turning to the conclusions he had come to after his conversation with Sophie. As the days passed it all seemed too fantastic. So fantastic, he dare not discuss it with anybody else.

Sophie hadn't mentioned it again. She probably thought he was over-reacting. Jack was beginning to think the SN technology had a bug. If the visitor counter had worked properly he wouldn't have got the idea in his head about aliens. He checked his domain regularly to see if anything arrived to explain how the game had got there. He began to think it was a promo gone wrong. He waited for an apology and an invitation to buy something linked to the game.

In the middle of the week, Sophie spent a day away at the photo-call with the rest of the team. The papers and screen programmes renewed their interest in her. Jack made sure he avoided any coverage of the Olympics.

Mr Donovan came to join them for dinner the next Friday. He carved the chicken and Mrs Donovan put the bowls of vegetables on the table.

"No champagne?" asked Sophie.

"We did that last week," answered Mrs Donovan. "You can have too much of a good thing."

"I thought we'd be having it every week, now," said Sophie.

"You know what thought did," answered Mrs Donovan.

The twins looked at each other and nodded. "No, Mum, what did thought do?" they asked in unison.

"Saw a dustcart and thought it was a wedding," she answered, as the twins collapsed in giggles.

"OK. OK. Behave you two," said Mr Donovan pointing the carving knife at them. "We'll have our next champagne when you've won a medal, Sophie."

"Four years then," said Jack and Sophie punched him.

"Calm down, Twinnies, please," said Mrs Donovan and prompted another fit of giggles.

"What shall we talk about today?" asked Mr Donovan once they were tucking in.

"Anything but the Olympics," said Sophie.

"But it's what everybody's talking about," her mother replied.

Jack remembered what they had discussed soon after the game arrived. "Any more stuff on what's happening to global warming, Dad?"

"There's been a bit more comment on it, Son." His eyebrows furrowed as he tried to remember what he'd read. "The scientists are flummoxed, frankly. Apparently, we're churning out more greenhouse gases than ever but the overall carbon dioxide level isn't getting higher. The carbon gases seem to be disappearing—"

"Into thin air!" interrupted Mrs Donovan.

"Yes. That's what's mystifying the scientists. It's got to be going somewhere."

"Are there any new theories, Dad?" asked Jack.

"Nope! Just the one about the supposed black hole. That doesn't seem to have much support. It's just a mystery."

"I saw on screen that the Americans are saying it's what they've been waiting for. It's the Earth's ecology balancing itself. It's happened naturally," said Mrs Donovan.

"It's the damn politicians saying that," said Mr Donovan. "I don't think the scientists agree."

"But, whatever the theories are, it's a good thing, isn't it, Max?" said Mrs Donovan.

"Yes. And there's more good news I read about this morning."

"What's that, Dad?" Sophie seemed pleased the subject was changing. She didn't want to talk about swimming but this science stuff was boring.

"Well, this was on the business pages…"

The three others around the table groaned.

"But I think it's something we'll hear more about," he said, ignoring their response. "An energy company in America has signed a deal to develop a new method of generating electricity…"

They all groaned again.

"No listen, it's a good story. They've bought the patent for a new process that super-freezes water. They said the ice it makes is as hard as a diamond. It compresses a litre of water until it takes up the same space as a diamond on a ring."

"You mean I could get a ring with a stone made of water?" asked Mrs Donovan.

Jack's eyes rolled upwards, he could see the impossibility of what his mother was suggesting.

His father was more patient. "Not really, Les. It would be so cold, you'd get instant frostbite, not just on your finger but probably your whole arm."

Mrs Donovan made a face. "What's the good of that then?"

"The interesting thing is what it does when it expands back to normal ice. It releases heat. And the key thing is it releases more energy as heat than it took to make it super-frozen in the first place."

Jack remembered his physics lessons. "That's not possible, Dad. Energy can't be created, can it?"

Mr Donovan answered, "That's what I thought. But apparently this process bucks the laws of nature somehow. It's all about the fact that the super-ice releases energy when it changes state to ordinary ice. The heat can be used to boil other water so it makes steam. The steam can be used to drive turbines. It's a very cheap way of generating electricity. All water-based – no pollution. The same water is used over and over again."

"Sounds too good to be true," said Mrs Donovan.

"If Amnugen Corporation has bought into it, they'll have made sure it works," said Mr Donovan. "They're one of the biggest energy companies in the world. They're behind it. Their people looked very pleased with themselves in the pictures. The guy who invented the process looks a funny bloke though."

"Why's that?" asked Jack. Even as he asked the question, the hairs on the back of his neck were tingling.

"Poor guy looks as if he's been caught in a fire. His face has been very badly burned by the looks of him. At first I thought the photo had been smudged. His features look as if they've been wiped away."

For Jack, the rest of the meal and the journey to his dad's flat passed in a daze.

As soon as they got to Mr Donovan's place, Jack asked to use his father's computer. He fired up his domain page. He called up hyper-search. He entered the word *Amnugen* and tagged the 'search' button. This took him straight to the home page of Amnugen Corporation. There was an announcement about the new process repeating what Mr

Donovan had said at dinner. There was nothing about the person who invented it and no pictures. There was, however, a 'more' button. Jack tagged it.

There was whole page on the new power generation method with a picture. It showed a group of smiling businessmen, all in suits. They were standing behind two men who were shaking hands. One of them was balding and quite fat. He was the Chief Executive of Amnugen. His smile looked forced. It wasn't surprising. Jack sympathised with him. It couldn't have been easy to spend time looking into the eyes of somebody who had endured the pain this man had.

Jack stared at the man's picture closely and the words, "You again," escaped from his lips. It was the man from the game. He was wearing a brown suit with a white shirt buttoned high up under his chin.

It was clear his burns were so bad he had to keep what was left of his skin out of the light. His hands were hidden inside white, cotton gloves. Jack wondered what the Amnugen man felt in his grip. The burnt man had no hair left and his skin was tight and papery across his cheekbones. His lips were gone and most of his nose was missing. His face was almost flat except for the hollows of his cheeks.

Jack read the caption: *Amnugen Corporation Chief Executive, Kelvin Harte, shakes hands with Professor Zavorus, inventor of the SERSI (Sustainable Energy Release from Super-Ice) process.*

Jack backed up to hyper-search. He texted: *SERSI.* There were a number of choices and he tagged the one mentioning the inventor's name.

The screen flashed and the grim face of the man Jack now knew as Professor Zavorus appeared. It could have been an enlarged version of the game icon.

Jack read the text: *Professor Zavorus, inventor of the revolutionary energy generation process called SERSI – Sustainable Energy Release from Super-Ice. Professor*

Zavorus has signed a deal with Amnugen Corporation of Grand Rapids, Michigan, effectively giving the company control of his invention. The company intends to build the first experimental energy generation plant in the city of Ludington on the banks of Lake Michigan in North America.

Jack skipped through some technical information on the process. He found what he was looking for at the foot of the page: *Professor Zavorus, 49, is a graduate of Exeter University in the UK. He dedicated his working life to developing a process for the sustainable generation of energy. He nearly lost his life in 2004, when an explosion caused a fire at his laboratory in the Lake District in Britain. He moved to the USA in 2006 for skin grafts and cosmetic surgery and resumed his work at his lake-side laboratory in Katonah in the state of New York.*

Jack wondered how he could verify the story about the laboratory fire in 2004. As far as he was concerned, Professor Zavorus was the man in the game. He tried to order his thoughts. Had he put Zavorus in the position where he could sign the deal with Amnugen Corporation? He tried to remember when he'd finished the game. It was less than two weeks before. How had Zavorus done so much in such a short time? He must have been around for longer. But if he had been, what was the point of the game?

Jack tagged back to hyper-search and texted in, *Lake Michigan*. He tagged on the first website on the list and read about the Great Lakes before moving on to Michigan itself. The first thing that struck him was the photograph. It showed a shoreline. It could easily have been the place where the man he now called Zavorus had walked into the water.

Jack closed down the website. His domain appeared. He glanced at it and saw something that chilled his blood. The burnt-face game icon was back. Alongside it there was another similar icon. This one had a combi alongside the face. It was asking Jack to get in touch.

Talking to Audak

Jack felt very alone. He tried to think back to before he'd seen the game. How much simpler everything was then. All he had to worry about was his sister's celebrity. He was convinced the strange man, Zavorus, had somehow come to life as a result of his actions. If SERSI fulfilled its promise, it would change the world. But Jack had the feeling that, like the game, the energy story was covering up something else. Now this new icon seemed to say he could talk to Zavorus. Jack's mind buzzed with questions. Why him? He was just a thirteen-year-old kid with a flashy computer. Why him?

His hand was shaking. He gripped his combi tight and tagged the new icon. A chat box appeared in the centre of his screen: *Connecting...* It was flashing and the full-stops pulsed like a promo hoarding. Jack had the urge to close the computer down. He wanted to run away, to get as far from this business as quickly as he could. His finger twitched on the combi. At the moment he was going to disconnect, new text appeared: *Hello, Jack. Thank you for making contact.*

Jack didn't know what to say. After a pause, he texted the first of the many questions spinning round his brain: *Are you Zavorus?*

No, Jack. I'm not Zavorus. You have made the connection between the game and the man who calls himself Zavorus. You are very clever. What else do you know?

Jack was angry. He wondered why he should have to explain himself. These people had barged into his life.

His palms were slippery with sweat as he texted furiously: *I know the game was more than it seemed. I know Zavorus is in Michigan because of the game. I know SERSI is not what everybody thinks*. It seemed too fantastic to add what he really thought, that he was to blame for Zavorus and he was terrified of what was going to happen.

The chat box responded without delay: *You have been clever to work it out. It is what we expected. It is why the man you call Zavorus chose you.*

Why do you say, 'the man you call Zavorus'? What's his real name? asked Jack.

We do not have names like you.

What do you mean? We all have names. Jack's thoughts were racing ahead, Not where you come from, you freak. You're from... but he couldn't bring himself to finish the thought.

Not where Zavorus and I come from. Each word hit Jack in the pit of his stomach as it appeared on his screen.

That's it. I'm going to shut this down. I don't want anything more to do with this. His cursor hovered over the closedown icon.

We need your help, Jack.

Something in Jack's head was stopping him tagging the icon even though every other brain cell was screaming at him to shut it down.

Why me?

Because Zavorus found you. Now we need your help to stop him.

It seemed like the earth was slipping away beneath Jack's feet. He was light-headed. The screen was growing in size. Or he was shrinking. He had to ask the question. He texted it into the chat box as quickly as he could. He knew it was too fantastic but he had to ask: *You are not from this planet, my planet, Earth, are you?* He cursed himself for putting it like that. "Just ask him if he's an alien, stupid," he said, hitting himself on the head. His mouth was dry as he waited for the response.

The chatbox streamed one letter after another. As each appeared, Jack experienced something like an electric shock in his chest: *No. We are from a different planet. It is a very long way away.*

Jack slumped against the desk. He wished his mum or dad was in the room. They would know what to do.

New text appeared: *We can go to vision now. Would you accept it?*

Jack texted: *Yes.*

But more words built in the chat box: *Please do not be alarmed by my appearance.*

The face Jack saw was similar to Zavorus's. The skin was green, not raw and pink. But his nose and lips were also burnt away.

Jack heard the man breathing. The hissing noise heightened the sense he was reptilian.

Jack spoke, "Does everybody look like you, where you come from? I thought Zavorus was hurt in a fire. That's his story. But, there was no fire, was there?"

The man's eyes changed shape and somehow Jack picked up it was equivalent to a smile.

"There was no fire, Jack." The man's lips didn't move. The voice Jack heard was the standard American sing-song of a voice synthesizer. "Let me tell you what happened. We want to be fair to you. I will tell you what you need to know," the voice said, while the man's hissed breathing continued in the background. Jack wanted to concentrate on the words but he was distracted. How was the man making the synthesizer work? He wasn't operating a keyboard.

"You are interested in the universe, I think," the man said.

Jack nodded.

"We know this because of your domain. Your species does not know how the universe is constructed. We have known for many of your years."

"How many?"

"Oh, Jack. Hundreds of your years. I will try to explain in terms you will understand. We know the universe is like a ball of string. But instead of a single strand it's made up of billions of strands, like elastic bands. They are bunched together to make a ball. What makes it difficult to understand is that the loops of elastic are stretching all the time so the ball is getting bigger. Does it make sense?"

"Yes, I think I understand." Jack's brow was furrowed with concentration.

"Now you have to think about one of the elastic bands that make up this huge space. You have something you call a Mobius strip. Have you heard of this, Jack?"

"Yes." Jack's mind was spinning with the thought that the alien knew so much about the Earth.

"You will know then it's a single strip of paper that's twisted before the ends are glued together. If you draw a line on a Mobius strip you eventually get back to where you started."

"Yeah, we've looked at them in Physics."

"Each of these elastic bands that make up the universe is twisted like a Mobius strip."

"But it's not solid like an elastic band, it's space."

"It is hard to understand. It would not be fair to tell you any more than you need to know."

Jack nodded.

"Can you remember where you are if you draw a line on a Mobius strip but only go halfway round?"

Jack pictured drawing the line in his mind. "You'd be back where you started but on the opposite side of the paper."

The man's eyes crinkled. "Good boy! Compared to Earth, that's where my planet is. On the other side of the strip. You can call my planet Consobrina. It is directly opposite your Earth. It is like being in another dimension. We could try to get to each other using the rockets you have on Earth. But, travelling along the strip, we would never meet because the elastic is stretching faster than your rockets can travel." He waited for Jack to signal he understood. Jack nodded.

"My people developed a way of travelling faster," the man continued. "We have reached the earth by going all the way round. It took a long time and our craft crashed and the occupants died. So we developed a way of crossing to your dimension from the opposite side. We can travel from our world to yours."

"Wow! How many people here, here on Earth, know about this?"

"Nobody, Jack. We estimate that, with your rate of discovery, your people will not locate our solar system for hundreds more of your Earth years."

"But, you've told me," exclaimed Jack. "I'll tell everybody. I know the secret."

"It's a risk we're willing to take, Jack. What I've told you is only a theory for you. Who will believe you when you say you've met an alien? You'll have no proof."

"But my computer?"

"We can wipe it clean any time. There will be nothing there. It's a risk telling you this but we estimate that, even if you become a physicist and spend your whole life searching for the dimensional solution, you won't make a breakthrough. It will happen in time but, we think, not in your lifetime."

"But what's all this about? What's going on?" Jack asked.

"For you to understand that," the man said, "I have to tell you about Consobrina."

Jack settled back in his seat. He hoped his father wouldn't disturb him.

The man continued, "Consobrina is not like Earth. One side of Consobrina always faces our sun. We have a light side and a dark side. The light side is land and the dark side is a frozen sea of carbon dioxide. Are you familiar with this gas?"

"Yes." The tingling on the back of Jack's neck started as he remembered the family's conversation about global warming.

The man continued, "Our atmosphere contains much more of that gas than yours. This means that the life form which evolved fastest in our world works very like plants do in yours. We are closely related to your trees!" His eyes crinkled.

"Our life form has three needs to survive: rays from our sun, carbon dioxide and water. Our sun shows no sign of becoming what you call a supernova. But we are using up Consobrina's resources of water and carbon dioxide faster than they can be put back. Our need for water made us evolve the ability to move around and not be rooted to one spot."

"So you had roots once. Like our plants."

"Yes, Jack. Many millions of your years ago. Our planet's water reserves are in reservoirs deep below the crust. There is a plant here with roots that travel many earth miles down to the reservoirs. These plants produce more water than they need for their own survival and the excess squirts out in a mist around them. There were huge forests of these plants creating an abundance of water. But the oasis plant is subject to disease. When a part of the forest died away, the other life it supported died as well. That's when one species of plant evolved the ability to travel on mobile roots to another forest so it could continue living."

"And you have evolved from that species," said Jack, his mind racing.

"Yes. Because we are like your plants, evolution is much quicker in our life-form. Normally we don't look like this…" the man used his gloved hands to point to his face and body. "I am part of a sub-species that was created to cross the dimension to Earth. This is as close as we can get to human form." His eyes crinkled again.

"But why is it important to come to Earth looking like us?"

"We thought it would be fair to you if our pioneers looked like humans." His head moved to dismiss what they had discussed. "I haven't got much time, Jack. Let us move on to what has been happening."

Jack's brain was spinning. It was already too much to take in.

"Our species has dominated Consobrina and we've been using up its reserves of the carbon dioxide we breathe. The sea of liquid carbon dioxide on the cold side of our planet is receding. Since we developed trans-dimensional travel we have been watching your planet. We have seen you have been killing it because you have too much of the gas we need. So we created a method of siphoning off your excess gas. We started this four Earth years ago."

"That explains what's been happening to the greenhouse effect."

"Yes. We created a dimensional portal over your North Pole and we are transporting frozen carbon dioxide through it to our planet."

"Some of our scientists have a theory that the harmful gases are being drained into some sort of black hole."

"What they call the black hole is the portal we created. They do not understand where the gases go because they do not know about our dimension. But it is good for you that we are doing this. It is saving your planet. You would have done nothing to save yourselves. If we had not intervened, your world would be on its way to extinction."

"Taking our gas is good for you as well," said Jack.

"I do not deny it. It is good for us too. We are in a position where our needs and your needs are roughly in balance. It is fair."

Jack registered the word 'fair'. The man had used it a number of times before. "Is being fair important where you come from?" Jack asked.

The eyes crinkled again. "Zavorus chose well," he said. "Yes, our society is built on respect for others – being fair. You are involved because Zavorus has broken this code."

"How?" asked Jack.

"Not everybody lives by our code. It is not easy to be a renegade because we communicate without speech. We communicate with our minds."

"Can you do that with me?"

"No! But we can communicate with you when you're asleep. We are able to make dreams in your head."

"That's how Zavorus got me hooked on the game, with a dream."

"Yes. But the game is not just a game."

"No, I see that now. But what did it do?"

"We do not blame you, Jack. You thought you were playing a game. Our people have developed the science of transportation. However, it needs powerful computers running programs at both the send and receive points. The program at the receive point is the more complicated of the two. Zavorus developed the game so someone on earth with a powerful enough computer could create the destination end of the program. It is not good for you he chose you."

Jack bit his knuckles. The plant-man had confirmed his worst fears. He looked at his watch. It was getting late. His dad would come in soon to say goodnight. He turned the sound down.

He lowered his voice. "Why did he choose me?"

"It was your bad luck, Jack. He could have chosen any earth person."

"Why did he come here?"

"Zavorus is a bad one. He is able to shield his thoughts from us. We do not know the whole story. We know his people devised a method for super-freezing water. It makes ice have the density of your diamonds."

"The plant in the Great Lakes."

"Yes. We think Zavorus is going to create a transportation point not a power station. He will super-freeze the water and transport it to our planet. Water in its normal form is difficult to transport. It has to be super-frozen first. Did you see Zavorus when he arrived on Earth?

"Was that when he came back together on my screen?" Jack asked.

"Yes."

"He was by a lake. Lake Michigan, I think."

"What was the first thing he did?"

"He went into the water." Jack said.

"The transportation process is very dehydrating. We need to get water into our cells quickly." There was a movement off screen and the man held up his hands so Jack could see them. He had taken off his gloves. Jack sat back as if he'd been hit in the face. He had expected to see something human-like. Instead each digit was merely a hollow stick like a straw. They moved stiffly when the plant-man put the gloves back on.

"We use these to take up water," he said.

Jack remembered seeing Zavorus walk into the water. He had taken off his gloves and had gone out until what Jack thought were his hands were submerged.

"So water is that important to you."

"We are like your plants, after all," the man answered and his eyes crinkled again.

"So if Zavorus is able to solve your water shortage by transporting it from Earth, his people will become very rich."

"He is doing it more to gain power for his people. Yes, he will gain from it."

"So you're trying to stop him."

"Yes. That's why we need your help."

"Why? Can't you get him back?"

"The transportation has to have a computer operating the correct program at both ends. Zavorus will never co-operate in anything that might bring him back to Consobrina while we are in power. I have to come to Earth to take him back."

"So you want me to play the game again?"

"Yes, this time to bring me there."

"But Zavorus's super-freezing process is good for this planet. It gives us energy for nothing."

"It does not work like that, Jack. We think super-freezing works as Zavorus says. There is an energy release when it thaws. But he will build plants all over your planet. They will all super-freeze water. The problem for you is that he will send water here. The loss of water will be greater as time goes by. It will put your planet in even greater peril than global warming."

Jack put his head in his hands and rubbed his eyes. "I did this. I brought Zavorus here," he groaned.

"You must not blame yourself, Jack. Zavorus could have chosen anybody. Your domain invited him to make contact. It is likely he has monitored your computer activity for some time to make sure you were the right person to play the game."

"What can I do?" asked Jack.

"If I get to Earth, Zavorus will have no choice. He will come back. All you need to do is play the game again. This time I will be transported. But you have to be quick, Jack. Zavorus will monitor your Web activity. He may already have picked up you have been researching Amnugen Corporation and Zavorus."

"How do you know?"

"We have been watching you since we were able to track it was your computer that ran the transportation program. We think Zavorus can only use Earth surveillance technology. We have better resources. We are trying to hide your computer from him. We don't know whether it will be successful. We will know when you start playing the game. You must start soon."

Jack thought about it. He was desperate to talk to an adult. He had to share this problem.

"I think I know what you are thinking, Jack. You are asking yourself, how can you trust me? I have no answer for you. You will be thinking that having two aliens on Earth is worse than having one. All I can say is you have to trust me. I have been fair to you and told you what is happening. You needed to know that. Think about it tonight. Please start playing the game as soon as you have decided. If you decide not to help us, please use the icon to contact me."

"You want me to trust you but you haven't even told me your name."

"You can call me Audak, if it will help you."

"What will you do if I decide not to play the game again?"

"We will have to find someone else," said Audak, as his picture faded from the screen.

Power Surges

"Are you OK, Jack?" It was Mr Donovan.

"Coming!" Jack closed down the computer. He wanted to think things over but he'd already spent too much time in his dad's study. He went into the living room. The light from the setting sun was coming in through the window overlooking the canal. The bare-brick walls shone warmly in the light. Sophie was stretched out on one of the settees. She was watching a band on the screen. The sound was off. She was listening through her earstud.

"Who were you talking to?" asked Mr Donovan casually.

"Just catching up with Luke," Jack said.

"Are you OK, Jack? You look worried about something."

Jack wondered whether he should tell his dad the whole story. But he couldn't see how he could make him understand what was happening. He considered what he might say, 'Well, Dad, it's like this. I'm in touch with aliens. Of all the people in the world, they've chosen me to help them. There's a bad guy who's tricked me into transporting him to America. Now there's a good guy, I think, who wants me to do the same for him. He says the world is in danger if I don't. What do you think I should do?'

Instead, he shook his head. "No, I'm fine," he said.

Mr Donovan glanced toward Sophie. She was concentrating on the screen. "Is it because of Sophie?" he asked.

"What do you mean, Dad?"

"Your mum and I, we both understand. It must be difficult to cope, with your twin sister getting all this publicity."

"I don't have a problem with Sophie, Dad. She deserves what she's getting." He tried to sound flippant. "It's a bit much when she's treated like a celebrity at the mall but I can live with it."

"The good news is, you won't have to live with it for long. She's joining the team at the beginning of next week. She'll be able to train in the pool in Olympic Park."

"I'm looking forward to going to London, to the posh hotel," said Jack.

Mr Donovan looked rueful. "It's costing an arm and a leg, Son. We have to make sure we make the most of it."

"Yeah," Jack answered. "I'm going to turn in, Dad. Is it OK?"

Mr Donovan gave him a hug. "Of course, it is. Try and get a good night's rest."

Jack touched his sister on the arm as he passed her on the way to the bathroom. She waved and they mouthed the word 'goodnight' to each other.

Jack's mind was crackling like a bag of popcorn in the microwave. His thoughts exploded and threatened to burst his brain. He tried to calm down so he could sleep. He really wanted to believe it wasn't happening. It would be wonderful if he could wake up with the calm knowledge it had all been a dream. But he knew this was his living nightmare.

He tried to gather in the wilder thoughts by applying logic: OK, this is real, he thought, Zavorus has chosen me because of my domain. I play games. Zavorus is a plant-man from a different planet. It's somewhere on the other side of one of the billions of expanding elastic bands that make up space. It's just my luck Zavorus's planet, Consobrina, is parallel to Earth.

He tried to keep the thoughts moving out one at a time in an orderly fashion: the plant-people on this parallel planet are helping us by sucking away our excess carbon dioxide – that's good. I've helped Zavorus get to Earth. That's bad.

Jack shivered when he thought of meeting Zavorus in a dream. Perhaps going to sleep wasn't such a good idea. He processed the thoughts again: Zavorus is a bad guy who intends to steal the Earth's water as well. He's going to pack it up in super-ice cubes and transport them to his planet. Audak, the leader of the good guys wants to stop him. He can only do it if I bring him to Earth to take Zavorus back. Audak can only get to Earth if I play the game again.

In Jack's tired state it all seemed logical. He knew, though, that, if he ever slept again, he would wake up thinking it would be best to not get any deeper into this thing. It would be best to try to forget it had ever happened. One thought kept pasting itself onto the screen of his mind: isn't it twice as bad to have two aliens stalking the Earth as it is to have one?

Jack woke with the sunlight battering the curtains. He was surprised initially, because his mind told him he hadn't been asleep at all. The alien face of Zavorus rose into his conscious thoughts. It was like a shark surfacing and a feeling of despair landed on him. He was still asking himself the same question he went to bed with: what should I do now?

He got up and walked to the window. A narrow-boat was passing by in the canal below. Jack opened the window so he could hear the engine chugging. The air was fresh and warm. The room filled with the green smell of the canal water as it frothed in the wake of the boat.

Jack's dad was having breakfast at the dining table in front of an open window. He too had a view of the canal. He looked up from his newspaper when Jack went into the room, "Hi, Jack. Sleep well?"

"OK," Jack answered before he poured himself some cereal and sat down.

"Look at that boat, Jack." Mr Donovan was smiling. "We should try it one day. They go along at four miles an hour. They don't have a care in the world. Lovely life."

"Yeah," Jack agreed. And if they have any sense they leave their combis at home, he thought.

"This is why I bought this apartment when your mum and I split up." Mr Donovan waved a hand toward the canal. "People like to live near water. It has a special quality. This property will always be in demand."

Jack preferred it when his dad didn't talk like a banker. "So you bought it because you knew the price would go up," he said between mouthfuls of cereal.

"Not just that," said Mr Donovan. "I always wanted to live near water. My ideal house would have a garden leading down to a river. A house with riparian rights, then you're talking."

"What's riparian?" asked Jack, his single eyebrow creasing in the centre.

"Riparian rights – it means you can fish and have boat moorings. It's like the stretch of river opposite your property belongs to you."

Jack didn't know how to respond so he stayed silent.

"Now, with global warming in reverse, if it continues, riverside properties will be back in demand. People like living next to water. You can't explain; it's a sort of primeval thing. We depend on water for survival so we feel better when we're next to it."

Jack groaned. "I've got to go out," he said and got up from the table.

As Jack left the room, he heard his father's voice behind him. "What did I say?" he asked. Jack was closing the bathroom door.

Jack went to the mall. He called Luke on his combi and Luke's locator told him he was in Birmingham. Jack remembered; Luke had said something about going to a cricket match. Jack was on his own. He wandered around the shops. Before he had left the house, he had arranged with his dad that they'd have lunch with Sophie. What should he do before then?

A couple of seats at the combi-point were free. They drew him like a magnet. He sat down and fired up his computer. The icons for the game and contact with Audak sat in the corner of the screen. They looked harmless but his hand shook as he moved the cursor.

I can start the game, he thought. It doesn't mean I have to finish it.

He tagged the icon. The familiar well-drawn buildings appeared. They glowed in the strange green light. Jack wondered whether this was what the parallel planet looked like. He studied the buildings to see if he could get any clues but there was nothing unusual. He looked beyond the buildings to the mountain landscape. It looked very like Earth.

Zap! Jack came to with a start as the screen faded. He hadn't been concentrating and the first zombie had got him.

"I'm going to have to do better than that," Jack muttered and tagged the icon again.

He started playing the game seriously and before long was sucked into the world of Zombietown. He must have been making slow progress because it wasn't long before the hotel icons started to appear. At first Jack ignored them, but after an hour he decided it wouldn't do any harm to save where he was.

He turned into the swing doors of a hotel and was in the familiar lounge. He walked toward reception noting the chair on his left. Jack remembered the shock the first time he'd played the game and Zavorus rose out of that chair. He turned toward it.

The movement, when it came, was slower, less threatening. Perhaps, Jack thought, it was because he'd been expecting something. It was Audak. He rose out of the chair

60

and walked slowly toward Jack as if his joints were locked with arthritis. He held up a gloved hand. "Thanks for playing the game, Jack," he said in his synthetic voice and the screen faded.

Jack tagged the icon to re-start. He left the hotel quickly and went back on the streets to zap the zombies. He felt he was doing the right thing.

The screen flashed. Jack's mind returned to the real world and he looked around. Had the mall lights flashed as well? He tried to recall whether the music had stopped for a second before droning on.

"Oh, no!" said the lady next him. "That was a power surge or something. I've lost my connection."

Jack's domain was on screen. He tagged the game icon. He was back in the hotel. Everything he'd done since leaving had been lost. He went back on the street. Almost immediately everything went dark. The background music stopped. The silence was eerie. Jack had never really noticed the mall's roof before. High above them its curved glass surface allowed sunlight to illuminate everything below in a soft glow. It wasn't dark but the lack of garish lights made it appear that way.

The music started up again and the lights flickered on. The music stopped and a chiming noise led in to an announcement. "There has been a breakdown to our local power supply. The back-up generators have started automatically and you can continue enjoying all our facilities. Please do not be concerned."

Jack returned to the game. He was back in the hotel reception. "Try again," he muttered as he went through the doors. Almost immediately, he was set upon by a gang of three zombies and he zapped them quickly. The screen flashed off again. Jack looked up. There was no sound, no artificial light. He sat patiently looking at the blank screen for a few minutes. The other people occupying the combi-point seats began to drift away muttering to themselves.

"Looks like that's that," said the woman. Jack nodded and smiled. It was what his mum would have said. The woman picked up her bag. "I don't think you'll be getting much more done here," she said to Jack as she passed him heading for the exit.

"…electrical fault. The mall is closing. Please make your way to the exits." Jack wondered where the announcement was coming from and then saw the security man. He was talking into a hand-held microphone and had a portable speaker on his belt. His amplified voice sounded again, "Please don't be alarmed. Please make your orderly way to the exits. There has been a power surge. It has caused our generators to develop an electrical fault. The mall is closing. Please make your way to the exits."

Jack went outside. It was too early for lunch and he wanted to play the game. He decided to go home.

Mrs Donovan was in the kitchen as he opened the door. "Who's there?" she called out.

"It's me – Jack."

She came into the hall. She was rubbing her hands on an old towel. Her hair was wet and stuck out from her head. Another old towel was spread over her shoulders. Jack noticed the final clue; her hands were encased in tight, latex gloves. She was 'doing her roots' as she called it.

"You're meant to be with your dad, Jack," she said as she reached up to kiss him. "You haven't had a row have you?" She took a speck of dye off his face with a latex fingertip.

"No. I needed to get something so I thought I'd pop back. I'm meeting Dad for lunch."

"Can I get you anything?"

"No, I'm all right. I'll make myself some tea and toast. Can I get anything for you, Mum?"

"Tea, the cup that cheers. One of those will do lovely, Jack," she said, leading the way to the kitchen.

He shook his head and followed her.

Jack sat in front of his computer and powered it up. He put the last piece of toast in his mouth and wiped his hand on his jeans before clicking the game icon. It didn't seem to have been damaged by the power surge. He started playing. He walked along the same street as before and dealt with the gang of three zombies. He was beginning to get in the groove again. He could already anticipate when the zombies were going to appear next and he was waiting for the first sight of the man at the window. Would it be Zavorus or Audak? He was making good progress.

The screen went blank and he heard his mum swear. She was in the bedroom next door. "What's happened, Jack?" she called. "My hairdryer's stopped."

Jack stood up, his mind racing. "It's all right, Mum. I'll check the switches."

He went down the stairs, through the kitchen to the utility room, picking up one of the kitchen chairs on the way. He stood on the chair and opened the box. It was as he feared; all the switches were in the 'on' position. It could mean only one thing. Something had gone wrong with the power supply to the house.

He raced back upstairs. He was breathless and it wasn't only because of the climb.

"There's a problem with the electricity, Mum," he said. "It happened at the mall this morning as well. They must be having problems with the supply. We just have to sit tight. It should come on again when they've sorted out whatever it is that's causing the problem."

His mum came to the door of the bedroom. The towels had gone but her hair was still wet. "I'm going out tonight," she said. She pointed at her hair. "I hope I can sort this out before then or I'll look a right mess."

"You'll be fine, Mum," Jack said.

"If it doesn't come back on this afternoon, I'll call your dad. He'll know what to do."

Jack was certain that, as long as he didn't play the game from the house, the fault would be sorted quickly. But how could Amnugen Corporation make these things happen? The company was huge but how could its tentacles stretch to the middle of England?

"Don't worry, Mum. I'm sure it'll be on again soon."

Jack wished he didn't need to worry. If Amnugen could prevent him playing the game, how was he going to stop Zavorus?

Audak's New Plan

"What's the matter, Jack? You seem miles away." Sophie sat opposite him and took a huge bite out of a pizza. Strings of cheese formed a bridge between her teeth and what was left of the slice she was holding. She broke them with a finger, wound them into a ball and popped it into her mouth. She was left with a smug-looking, close-mouthed grin.

Mr Donovan and Jack had met outside the restaurant, which was opposite the mall. They only had a few minutes to wait before Dan drove up in his battered car. Sophie stepped out and waved him off. Jack looked around and sensed heads turn in their direction when Sophie walked toward them. Some of the shoppers pointed at her.

Jack looked out of the window. He could see the mall. Its illuminated sign, 'Waterside' shone bright blue in the sunlight. The electricity was back on. Jack's mind turned to the people sitting at the combi-point. Some would be having a video-chat with friends, perhaps with relations in far off countries. Some might be doing research or even shopping on line. Going to the shops to shop on line, he thought, what a weird thing to do. A few might be logging in to their own computers as he had done. None of them would be sending a signal on to the Web that was monitored in America. None of them was in this totally random mess.

"Earth to Jack. Are you listening?" Sophie waved a hand in front of his face.

"Come on, Son. Snap out of it, as your mum would say. You're miles away today."

Jack willed himself back into the restaurant. "Sorry," he said. "I didn't sleep very well last night."

"Don't I know it," said Sophie. "I could hear you tossing and turning from the next room."

"You do seem to be distracted by something," Mr Donovan said. "If you were at school I'd say you were having problems there. We're OK aren't we?"

"What do you mean?"

"You're not annoyed at me for anything."

Jack cut off a bite-sized triangle of pizza and popped it in his mouth. "No, we're fine."

"Your mother, then?"

Jack sighed and took a sip of his soda. "Everything's fine at home, Dad."

The edge of exasperation in Jack's voice made Mr Donovan sit back in his chair. He shovelled a handful of salad leaves into his mouth.

"Must be me then, Bro," said Sophie and she punched him lightly on the arm.

"Will you stop that!" Jack snarled at her.

Tears welled up in Sophie's eyes. "What's come over you, Jack? If I didn't know better I'd say you've been taken over by pod people!"

Sophie and Mr Donovan broke into giggles. Sophie's imitation of her mother had been so accurate it seemed like Mrs Donovan was in the restaurant with them. The family had watched a movie in which aliens grew replica human bodies from pods. The only way to spot which humans had been taken over was their personalities changed. Afterwards, Mrs Donovan called the twins 'pod people' whenever one of them behaved out of character. Jack didn't even smile. Maybe the game was taking him over in some way. Perhaps he was becoming a pod person.

Sophie and Mr Donovan realised Jack wasn't joining in their laughter. "Come on, Son," Mr Donovan said. "Lighten up. It might never happen!"

It was another of Mrs Donovan's sayings and Sophie started giggling again. Even Jack was beginning to smile.

Sophie tried one. "Don't worry, Jack. It'll be a horse of a different colour in the morning!"

She and Mr Donovan spluttered and coughed as they tried to suppress their laughter.

Jack felt he should at least try, but he struggled to think of one. Then it came to him. "OK you two, I'm not as green as I'm cabbage looking..." He stopped. Everything seemed to take him back to Zavorus and that game.

He looked up and saw both Sophie and his dad were as still as statues staring at him. They could see the tears filling his eyes.

After the meal, the rest of which passed quietly, they went back to Mr Donovan's apartment. Sophie went for a nap and Jack asked to use his dad's computer.

"Only if it'll cheer you up, Son," he said.

Jack used his combi to fire up his domain. He gave the game a miss and tagged the contact icon. The chat box appeared and the word, *Connecting...* flashed.

"Come on," Jack clenched his fist. How long would it be before the electricity in his dad's apartment failed?

After a few seconds, which seemed a lot longer, words started to appear in the chat box: *It is good to hear from you, Jack. You have been having a bad time.*

Jack was in no mood for small talk. He hit the text keys: *Does Zavorus know everything I'm doing? Is he monitoring this?*

No, Jack, this channel is secure. He is monitoring your Web signature and he is picking up when you play the game.

How is he making the electricity go down? A new chat box appeared, *Go to visual?* He tagged the 'yes' icon.

Audak's face appeared. The familiar synthesizer started up, "He hacked into the energy companies' computers. He made selected circuits break. Your technology is quite simple for him."

Jack turned the volume down and whispered over Audak's wheezing breath, "How long can he keep it up?"

"We think that he can stop you every time you log in and create your web signature from now on."

"So, you'll have to find another way."

"No. Zavorus created the transporter game program to take him to Earth. It took him years. We were lucky to get hold of a copy from his people before they could destroy it. It is the only way for me to get to Earth. It may take us many of your Earth weeks to find another person to operate the program. Not many people have the SN technology in their homes. Your old PC technology isn't powerful enough. Zavorus chose you. He used dreams to make you one with the game. You can play it faultlessly. We have not the time to find anybody else. It has to be you."

Jack rubbed his eyes. All this was making him very tired. "It's too much. I'm worried that bringing two of you here will make things worse."

"I understand, Jack. But this is the only way. I can stop Zavorus but only if I'm on Earth with him. We have to get you somewhere safe. We can give you a new web signature. All we need is a place where you can play the game without being disturbed."

"Where? How?"

"We have been working on this since you had the problems earlier. We have discovered one part of your country that is secure. It has the latest protection systems for its communications and its access. We are trying to break into the systems now to get you the necessary credentials to stay there."

"Where is it?" asked Jack.

"The Olympic Park in London."

"Do you mean the competitors' village?"

"Not only the competitors' village – the whole park complex. It has the largest number of combi-points of any location in your country. You will be able to move around and play."

"My sister is a competitor. She will be there."

"Is that a problem for you?" Audak asked.

"No."

"Then we may try to turn it to our advantage." Audak's eyes crinkled.

"How will I get there?"

"We have new identity and travel documents in preparation at a number of locations but it takes time for us to get everything done. You will have bank and credit card accounts."

"How can you do this?"

"Your Earth computer programs are quite primitive. It is easy for us to hack in and change things. We can insert photographs and false backgrounds. It is what Zavorus did to create his identity. He made false records of his birth, his education and his research into super-ice. He has a false history. We could do the same for you but it is not necessary. We will create only what is needed."

Jack was suddenly struck by a weird thought. "Do you know how old I am?" he asked.

"You are in your Earth year fourteen. You have not lived long compared to many of your kind."

"I'm still a child. It isn't usual for children of my age to travel without their parents."

"We know this. We have compared you with others. We think it is possible for you to pretend you are four years older. Your documents will say you have seventeen Earth years."

Jack whistled. He was tall for his age and his voice had broken a year ago; but seventeen, that would be a stretch. "What about my family?" he asked.

"You must disappear, Jack. Not be traceable. We will arrange for them to receive calls to let them know you are safe. But you won't be able to tell them anything."

"When do you want me to go?" Jack asked.

"The security of the village is high by your standards. It is more difficult to falsify the documentation. We can do it but it will take a few of your Earth days. You will arrive in the village in three of your days' time."

"Tuesday?"

"Yes. Tuesday. We will have everything in place by then. We will arrange for you to receive a package with all the things you will need. You must leave as soon as you receive it. Your bank details and travel documents will arrive by post."

Audak gave Jack precise instructions on how to get to the Olympic Park and what he should do there. Jack started to make notes.

"I think it would be best if you try and remember how to do this, Jack. If you write it down you may leave a clue. You do not want to be traced. Do you understand?"

Jack nodded.

"If you follow this plan precisely we can make sure you disappear."

"How?"

"Closed circuit cameras are controlled by computers, Jack. It makes it easy for us."

Jack let what Audak had said sink in. "That's what puzzles me, Audak."

"What puzzles you?"

"If you can hack into our computers – security, banks, closed circuit cameras, why can't you make a computer run the game program for you?"

"As I explained, Zavorus has a great mind by even our standards. We don't really understand how the program works. All we know is you played it before. We have to do the same things again but I am the target this time. I am already in the send location Zavorus used. As soon as we know you are getting close to the execution part of the program, I will be ready. Our success depends on you."

Jack was blushing, something in Audak's face made him feel older, older even than seventeen. He couldn't think of anything else, so it seemed easy just to say, "OK. I'll do it."

"Thank you, Jack." Audak bowed his head before the screen faded and Jack was left strangely confident about everything that lay before him.

Jack went to the kitchen where Mr Donovan was cooking their tea before Dan collected Sophie. He was frying strips of chicken and Jack could taste the spice in the air. Fajitas was one of has dad's stand-by recipes. He often cooked it when they had a row to make up. Jack knew it was difficult for him because he had to make a non-spicy vegetarian version for Sophie.

Mr Donovan was wearing a T-shirt and shorts, which were hidden beneath a blue and white striped apron. His face was red from the heat over the stove and his dark brow was stiff with concentration. He took a drink from a glass of red wine. He was waiting for Jack to say something.

Jack wanted to talk. He needed to share what he was about to do. When Audak was on the screen talking to him, even though he used that impersonal voice, Jack was self-possessed and assertive. At the end of the last conversation Jack was ready to take on Zavorus and Amnugen Corporation single-handed. But, as the effect of Audak's presence faded and Jack pondered the complicated and fantastic events that surrounded him, he became diminished, younger, simply unable to cope with what was being asked of him.

Even with all these doubts about his ability to help Audak, Jack yearned to protect his parents from what was going to happen. Audak had said he would disappear. It meant his mum and dad were going to think he had run away. He wanted to warn them; to prepare them. But he also understood it was impossible.

If he told his dad the truth, what would his reaction be? He could imagine it. His dad would erupt with anger. He'd say Jack was making up this outrageous story to get attention. That he was doing it when Sophie was entering the most difficult period of her athletic life. Worse still, he'd be grounded and his parents would take his combi away. They'd probably be so annoyed they'd cancel the trip to London.

Jack could only watch his dad cooking and say what he was expected to say, "Having fajitas, Dad? Smashing, my favourite." He patted his dad on the back before turning round and going into the living-room where Sophie was watching a programme about the forthcoming Olympics.

Jack Runs Away

As soon as you get to London you will become Bradley J Gould. You are part of the British team. You are in the fencing competition. Audak's words appeared in the chat box as soon as they were connected. It was Sunday morning and Jack was using his dad's computer. He found himself shaking with fear and anticipation.

You must understand, Jack. Bradley Gould exists only as far as the Olympic Park security systems are concerned. You are not registered as a competitor in the fencing schedules. The British team managers do not have a Bradley Gould on their rosters. So you must keep away from them.

But where will I stay? texted Jack.

The competitors' village is governed by a different system. For that, you are a fitness coach attached to the American athletics team. It has reserved a large section of the complex and you have been allocated a single room there. Bradley Gould exists only for the village's security system. You will have to make up a different story if any of the American athletes or officials asks what you are doing there. You must invent something that fits the situation.

Jack gulped but couldn't think of anything to text back.

We will send you the clothes you need to look right in both parts. There are over 16,000 competitors and officials in the village. It will be easy for you to hide yourself.

Jack tagged the video icon and Audak's face appeared. Jack realised he was used to the featureless appearance. He no longer saw it as the face of a man whose skin and surface flesh had been burnt away. Jack's hands stopped shaking.

"I'll need money," said Jack. He was frantically trying to think of what else was necessary to make the plan work.

"You will receive envelopes addressed to Bradley J Gould tomorrow morning. You have a bank account and a credit card."

"What about ID?"

"That will arrive tomorrow also."

"Will I need a new Combi?"

"Yes. If, despite all our precautions, Zavorus discovers you are playing the game again, he could arrange for your base computer to be disabled. We have arranged for a new SN machine and a combi to be delivered to your accommodation in the village. It will be there when you arrive. It will be your new base computer. You will register the computer and combi as Brad Gould. This will create a new web signature and make it harder for Zavorus to track you down. As soon as we see the Brad Gould signature on the Web we will download the game and you will be able to make contact with me again."

"You seem to have thought of everything."

"We hope so."

"So next time I talk to you it'll be as Brad Gould from London."

"If it goes well."

"I'll do my best, Audak."

"I know you will, Jack. We do not have luck here but I think the right thing to say is, good luck, Jack."

"Thanks, Audak." As he closed down, Jack muttered, "I think I'm going to need it."

On Monday morning Jack stood in the front room watching the garden gate. He made sure he was by the open front door as the postman turned up their path. There were five letters addressed to 'Bradley J Gould', which Jack tucked into the waistband of his shorts and covered with his T-shirt. Mrs Donovan was in the hall when he turned round with the two remaining brown envelopes in his hands. "They look like bills, Mum," he said.

He took the stairs two at a time and went to his bedroom. He tore the envelopes open and threw the contents on his bed. He sifted out the promo leaflets and tore them up. He was left with three gleaming plastic cards bearing his photograph and the name, Bradley J Gould.

"ID, Bank and credit cards," he whispered. He picked up one of the cards and went over to the mirror. "Hi! My name is Brad Gould," he said. "Do you take plastic?" He offered the card to his reflection. "PIN number?" He glanced back at the letters on the duvet. "Yes, of course I know my PIN number."

He went back to the bed and looked at each of the remaining letters. One was from the bank and one from a credit card company. He had to remove a piece of metallic tape from each letter to reveal the PINs. Jack noted he had to register activation codes from all four letters with the companies' websites before he used the cards. He fired up his computer and carried out this simple task. While he was on-line he went into the bank and checked Brad Gould's account. Even if he saved all his pocket money for three years, he wouldn't have that much.

He checked the credit card letter again. His initial credit limit was enough to buy a small family car. It was all getting very real.

"Jack!" It was his mum calling up the stairs.

"Jack!"

He went on to the landing. "Yes?" he answered.

"I'm off to my gym class. I'll be back for lunch."

"OK, Mum. Have fun." He heard the front door close behind her.

He was on his own. He stood opposite the mirror again. He offered the ID. "My name is Brad Gould. I fence. Great Britain." His mood wavered between confidence he could look the right age and despair because he didn't look like an athlete. The security people wouldn't believe him.

"Hi! I'm Brad Gould. I'm one of the fitness coaches. Yes, I look young but it's because I'm so fit. Fitness like this takes years off you!" Jack laughed. Then another wave of hopelessness settled over him like a cloak.

He needed to talk to Audak again.

What if he talked to his Mum? Would she know who to tell? Would she believe him? He had some proof now – the ID and bank cards. But his parents would say he'd hacked into the banks' systems to create them. He had no alternative. He had to see it through.

Jack was in the same place next morning waiting for the courier's van. It was later, and his mother had already left for the gym club. It was too early for Sophie to be back from her last training session in Birmingham. She would be joining the team in London later that day. Tonight, she would be training in Olympic Park. Jack wondered where he would be.

He tried to imagine what it would be like in the house on the day after his disappearance. When would Audak send the first text to say he was OK? There would be a time when he was gone and his mum wouldn't know where. He wondered how his mother would take it. Would she send for his dad? Would they call the police? Audak had said they would be able to track him to London. Once he was there he, Jack Donovan, would disappear.

A brown van drew up outside. The driver jumped down, went to the back and opened a door. A few seconds later he emerged carrying three packages, two small and one the size of a large holdall. He carried them up to the door which Jack was already holding open. "Bradley J. Gould?" he asked.

"That's me," said Jack.

"Can I see your ID, please?"

Jack showed the new card. The man barely glanced at it. "Good. Sign here please."

The man held up an electronic pad. Jack started to sign with his normal signature. He remembered and swiftly converted the 'J' to a 'B' before finishing his new name with a flourish.

In his bedroom, Jack opened the smaller packets. The first contained train tickets from his local station to Euston in London and a day travel pass for the Underground. His knees started trembling. He moved round the room to get them under control.

The second, bulkier, envelope contained his security passes. They were white plastic cards with blue edging and they were attached to silver chains so they could be hung around his neck. One was for the Olympic Park and the second was for the Competitors' Village. Both had photographs of him, showed his new name, 'Bradley Gould' and confirmed he had 'Competitor access'. Each had a holographic bar code, which was printed over the Olympic symbol of interlocking rings.

There was a covering letter from the British Olympic Association. *Dear Bradley Gould*, it said. *We are sorry you are unable to attend the team meeting and briefing session. You will be able to pick up the joining pack at the Olympic Park competitor reception desk in the week commencing Monday 23 July.*

The joining pack contains all you need to know about life in Olympic Park and your responsibilities to the rest of the team. There is also an invitation to the team reception event on Thursday 26 July. We look forward to seeing you then.

These Games are particularly exciting and challenging for the British team. It is a home event for us and we are sure you will do your best to contribute to a record haul of medals. We know you have prepared meticulously for your event over many years and hope you arrive at the Games in peak condition ready to achieve your personal best. If this results in a medal either for you as an individual or for your team, so much the better.

With every best wish for your success. The letter carried the facsimile signatures of the captains of men's and women's teams.

Wow, thought Jack, Sophie will be getting one of these for real when she goes to the team meeting. He slumped down on the bed, the enormity of what his sister was undertaking sank in. They were both part of something huge.

The larger package sat alongside him begging to be opened. He tore open the plastic wrapping to reveal a large carrier bag from a high-street sports shop chain. Jack looked inside and found a blue and white sports bag. It had the Olympic symbol on the side.

Inside, Jack found three official replica Olympic tracksuits and five replica T-shirts. There were socks, also carrying the Olympic symbol, and a pair of the most expensive trainers Jack had ever seen in the flesh. Even he hadn't dared to ask his dad for a pair like it.

"Audak obviously thinks this is what the people in the village will be wearing," he muttered shaking his head. "I hope he's right."

There was just enough space to add a toilet bag and a towel before Jack zipped the bag up. He looked round his room as if it may be the last time. He patted his computer like he was patting a dog. "You started all this," he said.

Tears blurred his vision as he went downstairs and into the living room. On the sideboard was a framed photograph of the family taken before his mum and dad had split up. Jack was a cherub-faced child of about seven. He picked up the photo and crammed it in the bag. He checked one last time at the door: combi, clothes, security cards, tickets.

His mind flashed back to his room and he had a vision of the packaging and envelopes he had left in the waste bin. His mind zoomed in on an address label bearing the name, Bradley J Gould. He hurried into the kitchen and took an empty carrier bag from a drawer. He rushed upstairs and into his room. He picked all the envelopes and papers out of his bin and put them in the carrier. He didn't look back at the house as he turned out of the gate and down the street toward the bus stop.

The police pieced together Jack Donovan's movements before he disappeared. The lady who lived across the road remembered looking out of her window and seeing him leave the house sometime before 11.00 am. She told them she had seen a brown van pull up and deliver some parcels to Jack's house. When they checked this with the courier company which used brown vans, the police found there were no records for such a delivery. They thought the neighbour was probably confused. They didn't bother to talk to the courier company's local driver.

CCTV footage showed Jack getting on a bus at 11.07. He was dressed normally in T-shirt and jeans with a cotton jacket. He was carrying a holdall bag bearing the Olympic symbol. Sports shops had been selling bags like it in hundreds of thousands since before Christmas. He also had a carrier bag. The only unusual thing about him was he had chosen to wear his oldest pair of trainers.

The time he was next seen on the station platform was consistent with him not stopping anywhere. He caught the train to Birmingham and was filmed waiting for the London train. The CCTV on the train recorded him buying a soda and a chocolate cookie from the refreshment trolley. He paid with a five pound note. The holdall and the carrier bag were on the seat beside him.

Jack Donovan was next seen crossing the concourse at Euston Station in London. He went down into the underground and caught the first Victoria Line tube train heading south. He seemed to have bought his tickets in advance.

His underground destination was Oxford Circus station. Security cameras picked him up leaving the station and walking the few yards to the entrance of the Niketown store at 15.22. He took the 'up' escalator to the first floor and spent a few minutes viewing the Olympic exhibition. He then walked to the lift. He entered the lift at 15.28. The store's security TV system failed seconds later. By the time it was working again at 15.57, Jack Donovan had disappeared.

Jack had followed Audak's instructions precisely. Once in London, he made directly for Niketown. He paused in the Olympic exhibition on the first floor to make sure his presence was registered on the CCTV. He had an empty feeling in his stomach and wished he'd had something more substantial for lunch. He sauntered across to the lifts and pressed the up button. He got in and pressed for the third floor. He found the gents' toilet and went in.

All the cubicles were free. He chose the largest one at the end. Once inside, he changed into one of the tracksuits. He put on the new trainers and a blue baseball cap he found at the bottom of the bag. He stuffed his old clothes, the trainers and the carrier into the bag. He went back down in the lift and out of the store. He walked along Oxford Street to a cash machine and took out £100 pounds using the new bank card. Bradley J. Gould had come to life.

Olympic Park

By four o'clock that afternoon, Jack was in a taxi on his way to the Houses of Parliament. He walked across Westminster Bridge to the London Eye where he got into another taxi. "Olympic Park," he said.

The driver looked at Jack in the rear-view mirror. Jack could see his pale eyes and freckled forehead. His hair was gingery and thin and Jack noted the ginger fluff hanging over the collar of his shirt.

"Which entrance?" asked the driver.

Jack hadn't been prepared for this. "What do you mean?" It was the first time he'd spoken to anybody properly since leaving home.

"Well there's the big public entrance. That's to the south. I don't think it's open yet. It's by the huge new car parks. That's where you go if you have tickets to see events. Or I could drop you at Stratford International station. That's mostly for members of the public who arrive by train." He speared Jack with his pale eyes again. "Between you and me, us cabbies have been told we'd be doing a better job for our customers if we drop them there. Shorter queues and you're nearer the stadium and the Aquatic Centre. Not the other events, though. But it doesn't kick off until Friday." The eyes took him in again. "What are you doing there?"

Jack thought quickly. If he said he was a competitor, the driver might ask all sorts of questions. "I've got a job in the village," he said.

"What competitors'?"

"Yes the village for competitors."

81

"What are you doing?" The driver swore under his breath as a cyclist cut across as they were pulling up at some lights.

"Flipping burgers," he said.

"Not so glamorous, then."

"No," said Jack.

"Well, I know there's a restricted entrance to the east side for competitors. It's not far from the station. You'll have to go through security."

"I've got a pass," said Jack, delving into his bag.

"What say I drop you off there? If you don't have the right security, it's only a short walk to the entrances by the station and you can try there. Shall we do that?"

"Yes," said Jack, happy he hadn't given away anything to the driver.

"What do you think our chances are?"

"Pardon?"

"Medals," said the driver and again Jack was aware of his piercing eyes sizing him up. "How do you think we'll do?"

Jack realised he hadn't been sucked into the Olympic fever that had gripped the country. He'd been sitting in front of his computer for too long.

"I think we'll do well." He thought back to the competitors' letter. "If everybody does their personal bests we could end up with loads of medals, maybe a record."

"Mmm," said the driver. "I'm not so sure myself. I'd like to see that young girl get something, though. Sophie thingy."

Jack grinned. Even here he couldn't get away from it. "Donovan," he said, and his heart felt big enough to burst through his T-shirt. "Her name's Sophie Donovan."

"Yeah! That's the one. I'd like to see her get something. Not sure they should let them in that young though. Must be one hell of a swimmer."

"Yeah, she must be," Jack said.

They had crossed the river and were now alongside it on the north side. Jack could see the Dome ahead with its characteristic yellow struts. Each was flying an Olympic flag.

Shortly afterwards, the new buildings of Olympic Park stretched across the windscreen. The high silver curves of the stadium gleamed to the right and to the left a cluster of square white buildings which looked like apartment blocks shone in the sunshine.

"Nearly there. We've got to get round the other side," said the man and drove on in silence.

Jack ran his tongue across his lower lip. Both were as dry and rough as sandpaper.

The competitor's entrance to Olympic Park was protected by a silver arch, on which huge Olympic flags fluttered in the breeze. They snapped like loose boat sails. There was a faint humming noise as the wires supporting the arch vibrated with a tension Jack felt in his body. He approached one of the entrances.

There was an airport-style gate for him and a conveyor belt for his luggage. To his left a coach was off-loading a team from an African country and they chatted among themselves as they sauntered through the gateways. Jack could see that, beyond the gate, there was a bank of glass pods. The competitors stepped in one at a time and the doors closed behind them. They had to press a security pass against a sensor for the inner door to open. For a few seconds, each athlete was locked in the glass pod. Then the inner door swung round and they were free to exit.

The area was thick with security people. It looked like their main job was to make sure the machines were working properly. They hardly ever looked at the faces of the men and women passing through.

It was time for Jack to make a move. He took his park security tag out of the bag and hung it around his neck. He tried to look casual as he put his bag on the conveyor belt. It moved into the imaging device. Jack imagined what would be on the screen. He was confident his small supply of clothes and his washbag contents wouldn't set off any alarms. He went through the airport gate without any warnings being sounded – so far, so good.

He walked forward to the glass pod. The sliding door was open and he stepped in. The outer door closed behind him. He tilted his body to the right so the tag could reach the sensor. The light flashed red. It flashed red again. Then a warning buzzer sounded above his head. One of the security men looked at something above his pod and stepped forward. The light flashed green. The inner door slid open silently.

Jack was able to step out but a security man was blocking his path. Jack's face blushed with so much heat he started sweating uncomfortably. His legs felt full of sparks. He was ready to run.

The man was looking at the mini-screen on his combi. "Mr Gould?" he asked.

Jack's throat was so constricted he could only make a squawking noise and nod.

"Don't be alarmed, Mr Gould. That happens the first time you come through. It's so we can give you your accommodation pack. Pick up your bag and come with me please."

Jack pulled the sports bag from the end of the conveyor belt and followed the man though a door marked, 'Security Reception'. An envelope with papers was already waiting on the counter top. The security man went round to the other side. There were security men and women in the room wearing large flag pins on their shirt pockets. Jack assumed they indicated the languages that the attendants could speak.

The man with Jack, whose name badge said 'George' wore a single Union Flag pin.

"You already have your security tag for the accommodation building, don't you." George said.

Jack nodded.

"Good. That's one part of the operation working properly. When you go through the entrance to the competitors' village, they'll give you an envelope with details of your accommodation. That will also show the direct entrances into the village. You don't have to come through the park."

Jack nodded again. He thought a seventeen-year-old competitor would say something, but he couldn't think what it might be. Better to stay quiet, he thought.

"Can I have your main tag, please?"

Jack unwound it from his neck and George put it in a reader. Jack's pulse roared in his ears. It almost blotted out what George said next.

"Fencing, eh. What are your chances?"

"We'll I'll do well if I get to the quarter-final," said Jack copying his sister.

"Seventeen, you must be top man for your age," George said.

"Mmm. I've been very lucky," said Jack, trying to sound modest and convincing at the same time.

"Well, we're not meant to say this, but I hope you get a medal."

Jack was relieved George hadn't asked any questions about fencing. He resolved to find out more about it as soon as he had access to the Web.

"Right, it all looks fine, Mr Gould," said George. "Here is everything you need to know about the village. There's a cashcard in there. None of the outlets here accept cash or other plastic. You can put credits on the card at any of the multi-points. If you're lucky your team will give you an allowance."

He showed Jack to the door of the security station. "The British accommodation is to the left as you enter the village. There are lots of signposts, you shouldn't get lost." He shook Jack's hand. "Good luck again."

"Thanks," said Jack as he shouldered his bag. He went through the entry arch and puffed out a huge sigh. He was in Olympic Park.

He stood on a white stone walkway. Straight ahead of him a fountain was shooting jets of water into the air. Men and women in track-suits sat chatting in groups on the wall around it. Squinting against the sun, Jack turned to his left and saw the rippling roofs of the new stadium. It was much more impressive in reality than it looked on the screen.

Jack turned back toward the gleaming white apartment blocks on his right. The fronts glistened as the sun caught the metal of the balconies cascading down the front. Here and there, more athletes, many in vests and shorts, sat taking in the views.

Jack decided he should move. He didn't know who might be watching him. He passed the pool-table green pitches of the hockey centre on his left and strolled confidently toward the village. For the first time since he had got out of the taxi he felt in control of his life.

All around him fit young men and women strolled the white-paved pathways. Most of them were dressed like him in tracksuits. Many were in their national colours. Some jogged along, warming up muscles honed to peak condition. Other moved in groups, laughing and sharing a joke. Their easy friendship made Jack feel very alone. He couldn't afford to make a friend. His identities only worked for the computers that controlled the security of the huge campus. Friends would ask questions. They'd want to know about his place in the British fencing team or his role as a fitness coach. He could easily slip up. He'd be discovered.

The best thing to do, he thought, would be to get to his accommodation and fire up the SN computer straight away. He'd register as Brad Gould and start playing the game from the combi-points dotted around the park. If he played almost continuously, stopping only for meals and sleep, he reckoned he could be back home before the opening ceremony. He'd be missing for three days, maximum. He could go home and come back to London with his parents. He'd still stay at the swish London hotel. That's if they forgave him for running away.

86

The gateway to the competitors' village was controlled by a bank of glass pods identical to the ones at the park entrance. There was one security lady on duty. She had four badges: UK, France, Germany and Italy. Jack tried hard to look casual as he put his bag on the conveyor belt and approached the security pod. He wanted it to look like he had done this a hundred times before. He touched his accommodation security card to the sensor. This time he expected the delay. The woman stepped forward. She smiled. "Mr Gould?" she asked and held out a hand.

Jack decided to keep his talk to a minimum. In the Olympic Park he was Brad Gould, British fencer. Here in the competitor's village his security identified him as a US team coach. He wasn't sure he could carry off the accent. "Hi," he said.

"My name is Hannah," she said, pointing to her badge. "If you follow me, I will give you directions to your accommodation." Her voice had a sing-song quality that reminded him of Audak. "The security tag you used here," she pointed to the pods behind him, "Is the key to your room also."

Jack was worried she was going to ask for his main security tag. If she checked both of them in the reader, she'd see he had two identities.

She stood the other side of a desk. The envelope between them had the name 'Bradley J Gould'.

"Your accommodation tag, please, Mr Gould?" Hannah held out her hand.

Jack took the correct chain from around his neck and passed it over.

"That is in order, Mr Gould." She pushed the envelope across. "If you have any problems with your accommodation, please dial zero from your room. Each building has a concierge. For whatever you may need, he is pleased to help you."

"Thanks," Jack shook her offered hand.

"Good luck, Mr Gould," she called after him as he left the security station. He picked up his bag and went out onto the small square. Pathways went off in every direction. Jack suppressed the urge to punch the air but his brain surged with the elation of the moment. 'I've done it! I'm inside!'

Jack followed the directions that took him into the heart of the village. He passed other competitors along the way. They were alone or in groups. Few were wandering idly; each of them appeared to be on the way to something exciting. Here and there Jack saw the blue, red and white of a British tracksuit. He reminded himself to avoid Sophie.

He approached the building which would be his home for the next few days. The entrance was guarded by another set of security pods. This time he passed through without a hitch. Now he was amongst members of the American team. He reminded himself there were over five hundred of them. They wouldn't see him as a stranger. He just had to look as if he knew where he was going.

"Hey, Buddy, hold the lift!"

Jack heard the shout and quickly pressed the 'doors open' button. Then he wished he hadn't. It meant he'd have company for at least part of the way to the sixth floor.

A black man in an American team track suit stepped in. He had to duck to avoid the top of the doors and now stood with his head slightly stooped so his hair didn't brush the ceiling. Jack barely came up to the man's shoulder. Jack looked at his face. It was smooth and uncreased, without any evidence of a beard, and Jack thought anybody seeing them together might say they were the same age.

"Hey man," the American said and they shook hands the same way Jack did with Luke. "Not seen you around before. Where you heading?"

"Sixth floor," said Jack.

"You're a Brit!" exclaimed the man. "I'm Jim, Jim Priest. What you doing in the American team house, man!"

Jack thought quickly, it didn't matter what he said as long as it sounded sensible. Audak had told him that what his tags told the computers and what he told the people around him could be very different.

"There's been a mess up in the accommodation," he said. "I'm training to be a concierge. The top floor of this building isn't being used and I've been put in here for a few days until they can sort it out."

The man looked down on him doubtfully. "As long as you're not a spy," he said.

They arrived at the fifth floor. "This is my stop," Jim said, but he stood with one huge foot jammed against the lift door to stop it closing.

Jack tried to laugh it off. "No, I'm only here for a few nights. I'm starting training tomorrow so you won't see anything of me. I'm just here to sleep."

"How come you're so late being trained?"

"We've lost some people, I suppose. I've just been brought in." Jack could feel himself getting red and uncomfortable. "What's your sport?" he asked.

"Guess," said Jim and leaned back so his head bumped against the steel roof of the lift.

"Basketball?"

"Yihah! Right first time, Brit." He offered Jack a high five, which Jack had to get onto tip-toes to reach. Jim stepped out of the lift and the door started to close.

"See you round, Brit!"

"See you," Jack said and he could hear Jim chuckling as he made his way along the corridor.

The lift stopped on the next floor and Jack stepped out. He congratulated himself on his quick-thinking. Audak had told him the top floor of this building had been left empty, so it seemed plausible for the organisers to use it in an emergency. He was doing well.

He arrived at room 612 and pressed his tag against the sensor. The lock clicked and he pushed open the door. He was in a room with a single bed covered by a red and blue patterned duvet. There was an easy chair and a bedside table with a telephone. A desk was set up in front of the floor-to-ceiling window. Jack noticed immediately the desktop was clear. There was an empty space where there should have been a brand new, gleaming SN computer, ready and waiting for him to play the game.

Jack's mind was still reeling from the discovery that the SN computer hadn't arrived when the doorbell rang. How could anybody know he was there? He pressed the 'entry' button below the screen. He saw the image of a young man standing outside his door. He had a dark, neatly-trimmed goatee beard and wore a blue blazer like the people at security. Jack used the screen controls to toggle in on the man's badge. He read the words, 'Steve Walters, Concierge'.

Jack breathed deeply. He needed to get his racing mind and pumping heart under control. Had Jim, the basketball player, said something to the concierge, already? Surely there hadn't been time. Anyway, Jim had been on his way to his room. Why was the man at the door? Jack presumed the concierge had access to the security system. That meant he had to stick to Audak's cover story. But what if Jim had called to tell Steve Walters about the trainee concierge on the sixth floor?

Jack went to the door and opened it.

"Mr Gould?"

Jack nodded and stood back. The man stepped inside. His trousers were neatly pressed and his black shoes shone.

"Hi! My name is Steve Walters and I'm your concierge," he announced, bowing his head slightly.

They shook hands.

When Jack stayed silent, Steve continued, "I just wanted to welcome you to my building and let you know I'm here to help."

Jack's brow furrowed. "How did you know I was here?" he asked.

Steve smiled. "That's easy. My console downstairs lights up like a Christmas tree when somebody uses their room key for the first time. We want to make you feel welcome."

Jack resisted the urge to let out a big sigh. "Thanks," he said.

"To be honest, Mr Gould, you're a bit of a surprise package."

"What do you mean?" Jack's pulse quickened again.

"I was told the sixth floor would be vacant. I didn't expect you to be here. But the system had you down for this room. So you're very welcome." He looked at Jack as if waiting for an explanation.

"Yes... um. I've been sent over from the US – late." Jack was not at all sure he sounded genuine.

"Why's that?" Steve seemed sincere in his interest.

At that moment, Jack had no idea what to say. He raced through the bare facts of the cover story Audak had given him. He would have to add something - but what?

"Well... actually... I'm a new recruit to the coaching team." Would it be enough to satisfy the concierge?

"Why's that? Has somebody had to go back?" Steve's chin was pulled in and his beard brushed his tie. His blue eyes were openly questioning.

Jack was reluctantly making up his mind to pile yet another lie on to his already dangerously top-heavy story. "Actually... it's to do with my special job here." He was merely buying time. His mind cast around frantically for something to shore up his story.

Steve stroked his tie to make sure it sat flat beneath the lapels of his jacket.

Jack turned his back on the concierge and led the way into his room. "Come in. Sit down," he said, indicating the single chair. He still had no idea what to say about his coaching role.

Steve looked round the room as he sat down. When his gaze passed over the desk, he stood up as if the chair had been red hot. "Where's your computer?" he asked. "You should have a computer. Every room has an Internet-ready computer console linked to their screen. I'm so sorry. I can't believe we've made such an error. How are you going to do your... coaching, whatever, without a computer?" He was literally wringing his hands as if he were covering them with invisible cream. He stopped and checked something on his combi. "I'm sorry. There must have been a mistake."

Jack watched as Steve's face turned the colour of beetroot and waited for him to stop hitting the keys.

Steve looked up. "It says here," he tapped his combi screen, "your people asked for a room without a computer. Why would that be?"

Jack shrugged nonchalantly. He was in control of the situation for the first time since Steve had rung his doorbell. "I need an SN machine for my work – sending big files backwards and forwards to the US – so we've got one on order. It should have been here already, actually."

Steve leaned forward like an eager puppy. "Can I help you chase it up, Sir?" he asked.

"No, don't worry. I'll get my people to do it," answered Jack.

"If you're sure?"

"Absolutely." Jack led the way to the door.

"Well, if there's anything you need. Just call, or pop down. My desk's at the entrance to the residents' lounge. We've got pool, snooker, darts, combi-points – everything you need, down there."

"That's fine," said Jack. "But I'll probably spend most of my time working."

"Yes, of course," said Steve as they shook hands. "Well, goodbye." He took a last accusing glance at the space where the computer should have been and left.

Jack closed the door behind him and turned back into the room. He blew out a long breath and felt his spine relax. It had been as tense as a wire. He knew what his mum would say; it was one of her favourites: 'what a tangled web we weave when first we practise to deceive'. All this deceit was tiring him out. He wondered how long he could keep it up.

Calling Audak

"Maybe it'll be here tomorrow," Jack mumbled, thinking about the computer. He was back in the room after taking a trip to the dustbins. Once he had unpacked his few possessions, he was left with the carrier bag containing the evidence of his old identity and a bundle of clothes including his old trainers. He read the information about the accommodation and saw there were bins in a little building attached to each block. Taking a deep breath, Jack went back outside and dumped the evidence of Jack Donovan's existence.

He felt like a butterfly newly-emerged from a chrysalis. He really had become Brad Gould. Since jumping into the taxi, he had been a burger flipper, a fencing champion, a fitness coach and, lately, a trainee concierge.

That's enough identities, he thought as he lay back on the bed. I'll be the coach for Steve but I'll stick to the concierge story for everybody else. That way nobody's going to ask me about fencing. It'll be all right as long as I keep clear of the residents' lounge.

He could see it would be a real problem to run into Jim and Steve at the same time. The consolation was he only needed to keep it going for a few days. As long as the computer arrives, he thought. It has to be here tomorrow.

Audak had said it would be there when he arrived. What if he doesn't know it's gone wrong? Jack resolved to contact him.

Jack reached over and looked into his bag. The combi was there. He tried to remember what Audak had said. It's not secure, Jack thought. Audak said to wait for the new combi to arrive. He's waiting to hear from Brad Gould. He was worried Jack's combi could be traced.

Jack noticed something at the bottom of the bag. He had ignored it while he was putting his clothes away. It was the framed photo he had picked up before leaving. He set it upright on the bedside table and looked at it through blurring eyes.

He wondered what was happening at home. His mum would be unhappy he had disappeared on the day his sister was leaving for the Olympics. By now, though, she would be worrying. He hoped Audak had sent the message.

He was hungry. He hadn't eaten anything since the cookie on the train. He made sure he had his cards and tags and left the building once again.

The signs led Jack to a place not unlike the mall in his home town. It was set up beside a canal which had wide walkways on either side. There was a multi-point at the entrance. Jack charged up his cash card and went into the building. Men and women athletes milled around without giving Jack a second glance. They sauntered along in pairs or groups, chatting in their home languages. It was relaxed and easy but Jack was overwhelmed by his own solitude. He was in a place where only a few privileged humans were entitled to be, but he had nobody to share it with.

"Food," he said to himself and looked round. The mall was, in fact, a huge dining space on three floors around a central atrium. All the familiar restaurant chains had self-service counters on the perimeter. Jack spotted his favourite pizza place.

Twenty centimetres of pizza and a soft drink later, Jack made his way back to the room. The pathways were now thick with Olympians heading homeward and they accepted Jack as one of them. They neither took notice of him nor did they ignore him. He was just one of them. He fitted in.

Back in his room, Jack settled in for the night. He'd picked up a packet of dried fruit, the nearest thing he could find to sweets, and sat in bed munching them. He was luxuriating in the fact his mum and dad weren't there to make him clean his teeth. He dozed off watching the screen. It was a film about spies. Nothing like the real thing, was his thought moments before he slipped into a deep sleep.

The breakfast counter provided Jack with orange juice, cereal and a bagel with jam. While he was in the food court he was worried he might see Sophie. There were seats for over 5000 people there but, even so, he thought it possible they might bump into each other. He paid with his cashcard and hurried back to the room to await delivery of the computer. The magazine he'd bought took him through to lunch-time.

He picked up a sandwich for lunch and bought a book before returning quickly to the room. It's amazing how fast everything becomes familiar and you settle in, he thought.

He waited until five o'clock. It's not going to come now, he thought. There's only one thing to do. He was sure Audak said the line to him was safe. I can let him know the new computer and combi haven't been delivered, he reasoned. He sensed every day that went by was wasting time. The more time Zavorus had, the more powerful he would get.

Jack reached for his combi. He pointed at the screen and tagged the code. His stomach lurched as his domain flashed up. There in the corner were the two icons. Still reeling from the emotional high of seeing the familiar screen again, Jack tagged the one for communication.

The screen flashed and he was in the green-tinged townscape of Zombietown. "What the…!" Jack exclaimed. His mind thrashed about for an explanation, "What's happening! It's the game!" Then, with dread realisation, he said, "You fool. You hit the wrong icon."

It was exactly what Audak had told him not to do. His signature was out there on the Web. Jack's mind raced, what's the quickest way to get out? As if in answer, the first of the zombies appeared in view. Instinctively, Jack reached for his gun. Then he realised, the fastest way to exit was to be wiped out. He let the zombie fire. A bright flash engulfed the screen and Jack was out of the town and back at his domain. He could only have been in the game for seconds. But was it enough for Zavorus?

Jack took great care to tag the correct icon for communication with Audak. The chat box appeared. He waited. Finally, Audak's text came through: *Jack, what are you doing?*

I had to call you. Jack hit the buttons as quickly as he could. *You said this channel is safe.*

Yes. But you started the game. We saw your web signature.

I was stupid. I tagged the wrong icon. Jack's skin burned at the thought even though no one could see him. *Will Zavorus have spotted it as well?*

Your signature was there for only a very short time. I hope his surveillance is not as sophisticated as ours. You will be safe as long as he was not able to trace it back to your location. Why are you using your base machine again?

There's a problem. The new computer and combi haven't arrived yet.

We wondered why you had not started to play the game.

Jack accepted vision and watched Audak appear. "What's gone wrong?" Jack said smiling. It was good to see Audak's face again.

"We have checked the supplier's records," Audak said in the synthesizer voice. "The delivery was made on the day before yesterday. The day you arrived. The technician has confirmed the machine is installed and ready. It was tested as compatible with the screen settings and is linked to the combi that was delivered at the same time."

"It's not here." Jack switched to remote camera, held his combi up and twisted it round slowly so Audak could see for himself.

"We will investigate. We will try and make sure the delivery happens tomorrow."

"Is everything else all right?" asked Jack.

Audak crinkled his eyes. "I think you mean to ask, Jack, whether we have notified your family you are safe. We have sent them an untraceable mail from your combi telling them you have gone to London for a short time and are safe. They have called the police. This is understandable. You are only thirteen earth years old."

"But they're OK?"

"Yes. The police traced you to the Niketown store as we knew they could. We disabled the CCTV in the building as soon as you were in the lift. You are to be congratulated on following our instructions. We will keep sending messages to your parents for you."

"What do I do now?" asked Jack.

"You cannot do anything. Call me at this time tomorrow if the computer has not arrived. Please start playing the game as soon as it comes. We have to stop Zavorus before he does too much damage."

There was nothing else to say. The screen went blank and Jack was back in his domain. It suddenly looked dangerous as if it were betraying his position to Zavorus. He closed it down and switched off the screen.

All the next day Jack waited in his room. He watched the screen listlessly. The Olympic Park channel featured interviews with athletes and he wondered if he might see Sophie. He assumed the British team were keeping her out of the media spotlight. When he left the accommodation building for his meals he wandered along pathways, which were becoming more crowded. The tension was reaching a peak. It was the day before the opening ceremony. All the people around him were focused on their single purpose. How he wished he could do the job Audak wanted and get out of his lonely room. But Jack's bedside phone didn't ring and no delivery men came to his door.

This time, Jack was careful not to tag the game icon. He paced across the room while the connection was made.

I am sorry, Jack. There has been a problem at the warehouse. We may have caused a computer malfunction. All the deliveries for the same day as yours were affected. We have had to input your order again. It is now scheduled for delivery on Monday.

Jack groaned. I'm going to be stuck for three whole days in this room, he thought.

He texted: *What about Zavorus?*

The plant will take many months to build so there is no imminent danger. However, it would be wrong for your people to learn too much from what he is doing. It is putting technology in your hands that may be harmful to us. Every day is important. We have to be patient.

Jack tagged 'yes' to vision and the Audak's scarred features appeared. Jack returned the alien's crinkled-eye smile.

"We did not make an allowance for the poor state of the systems in one of your important companies. We are still learning about you."

Jack's smile broadened. He understood this was as close as Audak would get to a joke.

"Did Zavorus pick up my Web signature yesterday?"

"Not as far as we know."

"Do I have to stay here?"

"Yes. This location has the highest level of security for access and systems that we have encountered. It was quite difficult for us to get you in. Even if Zavorus locates you when you are playing the game, he will find it very difficult to stop you. He will not be able to interfere with the electricity supply as he did last time."

"But, I'm on my own here. I can't talk to anybody in case I blow my cover."

"What do you mean?" Audak said in his synthetic voice.

"If I talk to people they'll ask what I'm doing here. They may get suspicious."

"I understand. You are saying you need someone to talk with?"

It seemed a bit wet for Jack to admit this outright so he stayed quiet.

"Your sister is there."

"But, she's in the British accommodation. It's on the other side of the campus. If I meet her, how can I explain what I'm doing here?"

"Can she be trusted?"

"Yes, she's my sister."

"Would she tell your parents where you are?"

Jack thought about it. She would if she saw him and he didn't have a chance to explain. If he could make her understand what was happening, then she probably wouldn't.

"If I had time to explain, I don't think she would," he said. "Me being here with the security tags and everything. It would show her I'm being helped."

"Perhaps we can find a way of helping you to convince her."

"What do you mean?"

"You will see." Audak's expression didn't change. "Do you need anything, Jack?"

Jack thought about it. He had more money than he knew how to spend. His basics were all sorted out. He looked across to the family photograph. "No, nothing," he said. His voice sounded flat and hollow. Then he added, "What's happening at home?"

"Your mother and father seem to be reassured by your texts. The police activity has stopped. Your parents have cancelled their hotel booking. They have left a note on your domain. They say they are staying at home until you get back. You have a number of messages from your friends asking what you are doing."

"Can I see them?" Jack leaned forward.

"As soon as you leave your domain page, except for this channel, you are sending your web signature out for Zavorus to see. It will make it easier for him to locate you."

"I understand," Jack said, slumping his back against the pillows.

"We are worried this channel is not totally secure. You must use it again only for communication if the computer does not arrive on Monday. Until then you must do your best to stay beyond detection. If you find you can contact your sister without putting yourself in danger of being discovered you should make use of it."

"I'll stay in this building except for meals. So I won't be able to make contact with her without giving myself away."

"Exactly." Audak's face didn't change. "Contact us next using the new computer."

Jack turned away from the blank screen and buried his head in the pillow. "A whole weekend of this," he said, beating his fists into the soft mattress.

Sophie's Swim

The room was dark. It was the same as Jack's but the furniture was the wrong way round. The bathroom was to his left, not his right. The screen flickered with a pale light, illuminating two single beds. Jack tip-toed around the near bed. Only a tousled mass of blonde hair indicated the identity of its occupant.

Jack squatted down by the second bed so Sophie's face was only inches away from his. In the light from the screen he could make out her upper lip moving in time with her breathing.

He put out his hand and touched her forehead. His palm felt a surge of heat. It was as if he'd touched a sun-baked stone. The pain woke him up. His hand tingled with the memory of it. He had a headache. He slipped off to sleep again.

It was the morning of the first day of the 2012 Olympics. Jack was aware of it as he surfaced from his sleep. The swimming events were scheduled to start straight after the ceremony. Sophie would be swimming that evening. Perhaps, he thought, it's why I've got this strange wet feeling.

Jack's skin felt like it had been plunged into a cool bath. He could feel a peculiar wetness around him. At the same time, he felt powerful. His shoulders, arms and legs were bursting with unused energy. It was as if he was emerging from a long illness and, although he was still on his sick-bed, his muscles felt new again. He was relieved when the feeling started to fade and his skin lost its ghostly clamminess.

The walkways of the competitor village buzzed with excitement as Jack strolled to the breakfast counter. He felt a tap on his shoulder and turned round, alarmed. He found himself facing the chest of a much taller man.

"Hey, Brit. Remember me?"

"Jim," Jack answered. "Basketball man." They shook hands.

"You still living on the empty floor above me?"

"Yep, I'm still there. They should be moving me to the proper accommodation soon, though."

"How's your training going?"

"There's a lot to learn but I'm picking it up."

"Well, I've been learning all I need to know just by walking around," said Jim. "I don't reckon I need help."

Jack was keen to change the subject. "Are you going to the opening ceremony?"

"Yeah! We'll all be there. It's the end of everything."

Jack looked up into Jim's face, surely he meant the beginning?

"It's the end of all the uncertainty," Jim said. "All the training. All the hoping. Will I make the squad? Is my form good enough? Will I be injured? It's the end of all that. I'm here now. After today, they can't take it away from me." He puffed out his chest and it nearly hit the end of Jack's nose. "I'm an Olympian. Whatever happens after today, I can say that. I'm an Olympian."

Jack wondered if Sophie was thinking the same way.

"Anyway," said Jim, "I'm heading for training. You look after yourself."

They shook hands and Jack was engulfed in loneliness once again as Jim walked away.

The breakfast counter was doing good business. Jack took his tray to his usual spot by the window. He could watch the athletes jogging by. He thought about what Jim had said. Did his sister see it the same way? Is it the end of a long hard road for you as well, Sophie? he asked.

"What?" It was Sophie's voice. Jack looked round. Oh no! What's she doing here? My cover's blown, he thought.

"What?" He heard it again. This time he realised it wasn't a noise he was hearing through his ears. It was inside his head.

"Sophie?" He didn't say it.

"Jack?" Jack couldn't work out where the voice was coming from. His brain threw another thought out, "What's going on?"

He heard Sophie's voice inside his head again, "Jack?"

This time he thought it consciously, "What's going on?"

Her voice came through again. It sounded as if she was talking normally there in front of him, but she wasn't. "What? Jack? What's happening?"

His ears weren't picking sounds up. But his brain was receiving something. Sophie asked him a question.

He concentrated on sending her a thought, "Can you hear me?"

"Jack. How did you get in here? Where are you? You shouldn't be in here. How did you—"

"I'm not. I'm not there."

"Jack, I'm getting a really bad feeling. Will you tell me what's going on?"

"I don't know, Sophie," he projected. "I can hear your thoughts... I think."

"What? Are you crazy?"

It occurred to Jack Sophie might be speaking aloud. "Are you talking?" he thought.

"Of course I am, can't you hear me? I'm as loud as can be. People will think I'm crazy. Come out. It looks like I'm talking to myself."

"Stop talking," Jack sent. "Just think what you want to say and send it to me."

"Send it? You are crazy. Come out. Let me see you."

"Did you say that last bit?"

"What? Unless you come out, Jack. I'm leaving. How did you get here, anyway?"

"You didn't say that last bit, did you, Soph? You didn't say, 'How did you get here anyway?' You just thought it."

"I don't know what I said. Did I say it? I can't remember."

"I heard all that, Sophie. Not knowing whether you said it or not. You don't have to say anything. I don't know how but I can hear your thoughts."

Jack stopped thinking about what was going on inside his head and looked round. He had been concentrating so hard he wondered whether he'd been talking aloud. The people around him were taking no notice.

Sophie's voice appeared in his head again, "This is just the most awful thing that can happen to anyone."

After some more garbled messaging they agreed they did appear to be transferring thoughts to each other. They had to work out what it meant. Jack didn't tell her where he was. He asked when she had some time she could spend in her room so they could try to talk through their minds again. They agreed they would make an effort not to think about the other until that time. That way they would see whether their thoughts transferred only when they wanted.

That afternoon, when Sophie should have been taking her nap, Jack called out to her in his mind.

"Yes! Jack, is that you? This is the craziest thing. What's happened to us? It's my first heat this evening. This is all I need. No, it's the last thing on earth I need. My brother suddenly inside my brain talking to me. Are you crazy? Am I crazy? What's going—"

"Whoa! Sis! Please—"

"Stop that, Jack! This is the stupidest, craziest, most random thing that could happen to a person. It's happened on the most important day of my life. I'm entitled to feel just a little crazy, yeah? This is just so unfair."

"I think I know what's going on, Soph. I've been thinking about it all morning. But I have to tell you the whole story.

It's going to take a while so you're going to have to calm down."

"Calm down? Calm down! I'm meant to be preparing for the most important race of my life and instead I've got my brother's voice rattling around my head. That's no reason to calm down. It's a reason to go flip-out, totally crazy."

"Yeah, well, perhaps 'calm down' wasn't the right phrase to use. How about you not thinking anything for a bit? Give me a clear space to send some thoughts."

"Well if you think you know what's happening, clever-stick brother of mine, you try and tell me. It better be good."

"Did you have a dream last night, Soph?" he asked.

"Yes. It was about you, actually." Jack could tell she was sulking.

"Where was I?"

"You were in a room. Like my room here in the village. You were asleep and I touched your head. It was so hot I felt like I burnt my hand."

"And then you woke up?"

"Yeah."

"I had the same dream, only the other way round. I came to your room. I think that's when it happened. Look, you should know, I'm here in the Olympic Village. I'm staying in the American team apartments."

"Now you really have flipped, Jack."

"Sophie, calm down, please. I'm going to try to explain how I came to be here. I think it will help you understand what's happening to us. But it's a madly fantastic story. You're going to have to believe this is all the truth." He waited. "Sophie, are you listening?"

"Yes, I'm here. Go on."

"I've been in contact with aliens."

"What! You're totally mad. You are so far gone…" Sophie's voice trailed off in a storm of flashing thoughts Jack couldn't keep up with.

"Whoa, Soph. Please, please. Perhaps that wasn't the best way to start. I'll go back to the beginning. You remember I told you about that game? When you were sunbathing in the garden?"

Sophie did the brain equivalent of nodding and Jack took her through his story. She was silent. The more Jack sent his explanation the more incredible it sounded. If he didn't know it was true, he wouldn't have believed it himself. He ended by telling her how the SN computer hadn't been delivered.

When he finished, it took a while for Sophie to respond. Jack waited.

Finally her thoughts came through, "Jack, that's the biggest load of rubbish I've ever heard in my whole life."

"But you didn't hear it, Soph. I mind-transferred it to you. That's the point, isn't it? If it was all nonsense, how do you explain this brain thing we can do?"

"I don't know."

"Look, I've got an idea," Jack sent. "Tag this number." He gave her the number of Brad Gould's combi.

"OK…"

Jack's new combi buzzed. He picked it up and spoke, "What does the ident say, Sis?"

"Bradley J Gould."

"There, how can I have that? It's not stolen. I've got ID, bank account, credit cards…"

He closed the combi. "You still there?" he asked in his mind.

"Yes."

"Do you believe me now?"

"But how did you get into the village? What about the security?"

"The people – the plant-people from Consobrina – they seem to be able to interfere with our computer systems whenever they want. They set this whole thing up by hacking into computers."

"So now you're waiting for a new SN computer to be delivered?"

"And it doesn't come until Monday."

"And when it comes you play the game for a couple of days and leave?"

"Yes."

"So what are you doing until then?"

"I'm kicking my heels. At least that's what Mum would call it." As Jack sent this thought he felt a pang in his chest that seemed magnified by being in touch with Sophie.

"And you think this Audak's done this to us so you've got somebody to help you if you need it?"

"He said he would try and think of a way of getting you involved."

"But this, this is totally crazy."

"But we've used it for nearly an hour now. It's helped me. I feel better knowing I can talk to you if I need to."

"I can understand that, Jack. But it's not helping me – my preparation for the race."

"Sorry!"

"It's too late now. How do you think they did it?"

"Audak told me Zavorus was able to influence my brain while I was asleep. Maybe Audak's people have activated something in our brains we've never used. They say we only use ten per cent of our brain power. Maybe you and I are now using part of the ninety per cent that's extinct."

"The whole thing's totally off the planet, Jack."

"I'm afraid that's true – literally."

"What about Mum and Dad? I've spoken to them loads of times since I've been here. They haven't said anything about you going missing."

"They probably didn't want to worry you. Have you asked to speak to me?"

"You've always been out. I suppose I never thought about it. I was really annoyed at you for not being there when I left."

"I'm sorry about that, Sis. You can understand why now."

"Yeah. So what happens next?"

"Well you win your race this evening, Soph. Try not to think about this."

"I've got no chance of forgetting this, Jack."

"Sorry, Well, do your best, eh?"

"What about you?"

"I'll be OK. I'll be watching you. Good luck."

"Yeah. You too."

"Soph?"

"Yeah?"

"You won't say anything about this to Mum or Dad, will you?"

"Not if you don't want me to."

"Thanks, Sis. Good luck for tonight."

The noise from the stadium wafted in the open window of Jack's room. The speeches were followed by music that swirled in the breeze as Jack watched on screen with the sound off. He mulled over his mind conversation with Sophie. He was sure Audak was responsible. Knowing he could contact his twin had made this thing seem a lot brighter.

At the end of the ceremony the action started in the Aquatic Centre. Jack turned the sound up so he could hear the commentators. They were discussing Sophie's chances.

Sharron, the retired international swimmer, spoke with authority. "She's a very accomplished young athlete. Her achievement getting here is phenomenal. But this is not her year. Sophie Donovan is a gold medal prospect for Johannesburg. Not this time. She'll do well to get through this heat. She's had a tough draw. Five of these swimmers have faster Personal Bests than her."

"But with the home crowd behind her, Sharron?" asked the anchor man.

"If she's doing her job properly, she'll blot out everything but her performance. When you're in the pool you spend most of the time with your ears under water. It's a strange world. All the crowd noises are submerged beneath the sound of your own breathing. You can almost hear your own heart beat. You hear the movement of your body through the water. You get the rushing sounds from the strokes of the other competitors. Nothing can help you when you're in the pool. You're on your own."

Jack sighed. He wiped his palms on the duvet cover. He wished he'd been able to buy some chocolate.

They cut across to the pool and the first face they focused on was Sophie's. She was pale and her lips looked blue. Her skin was taut across her cheekbones.

Jack punched the air.

The camera panned across the other competitors. They seemed to have their brains frozen away in another place. The only thing that mattered for them was to distil thousands of miles of training into the next one hundred metres – two lengths of the pool.

"On your marks."

The swimmers tensed on their podiums, still as statues.

"Set."

Arms swooped back, they pitched their bodies forward, teetering.

"Crack."

Eight bodies launched forward as one. They cut into the water together. A V-pattern started to form with the American girl in lane four leading them. Sophie, in lane seven, was already falling behind. Only four would qualify.

At the turn, Sophie was in sixth place and the commentator was already talking about her brave performance. Then, imperceptibly at first, then noticeably, she began making up ground on the swimmer in the lane outside her. Halfway up the pool she was in fifth place. It was as if she were being dragged along by the German girl inside her, who was now challenging for third place.

"Keep going, Sophie! Go girl! Go on!" Jack was on his feet screaming at the screen.

It looked as if Sophie were attached by a rope to the German swimmer. As she challenged for second place in the final few metres, so Sophie slid into fourth beside her. Fourth place! She'd qualified for the quarter-finals!

"Yes! Yes! Brilliant!" Jack was leaping about the room like a crazy man. His twin sister was a true Olympian.

Jack Discovers Fencing

The walls of Jack's room seemed to close in on him. His sister waved to the crowds around the pool and walked off with a British team robe draped over her shoulders. Jack thought about his mum watching on the big screen in their living-room. His dad was probably in the pub by the canal lock standing his friends a round of drinks and being slapped on the back in congratulation. I wonder whether they're thinking about me, Jack thought. The cream walls of the room were now grey in the fading light. He was hungry and alone. He decided to go out.

He took the path to the food court and stopped by a burger counter. He sat alone at a table eating his chicken sandwich and fries while around him athletes in track suits were sharing stories of the early events. There was an excited hush as the American swimmer who had won Sophie's heat sauntered past. Jack looked down at his soggy sandwich and pushed another handful of fries into his mouth. He knew what his mum would say about his diet.

Most of the screens were showing events from the Olympic Park. Swimming was still on and boxing had started in one of the arenas. The screen above Jack showed the schedule of events and he was struck by something happening the next day. The fencing competition would start in the multi-sport arena at noon.

The room was dark. The screen had closed down. The first day's events were over.

"Sophie, are you awake?" Jack pictured Sophie in her room and thought the words in his mind. It was easier with his eyes closed.

"Jack?"

"Yes. Can you tal…" Jack realised they'd not yet thought up a word for what they were doing. "Can you do this? Now, I mean."

"Yes. I'm in bed. I can't sleep. Sue's given me a sleeping pill but it's not had an effect yet. Did you see it?"

"You were brilliant, Soph. Did you know you'd qualify if you hung on to the German?"

"I was just going as fast as I could. It was difficult to see where I was in the last fifty metres. The others I was worried about were right over on the other side of the pool."

"Anyway, you were brilliant."

"Jack." Sophie's thoughts came through tentatively. She was hesitating. "Jack. Mum and Dad called me after the race."

"Omigod! Oh no! You didn't, did you? Say anything about me?" The thoughts tumbled out before Jack had framed them properly.

"No. Calm down."

"Sorry."

"They haven't said anything to me about you disappearing so I can't mention it, can I?"

"I suppose not."

"It was a bit strange, though. They were both in Dad's apartment. I didn't think Mum ever went there."

"So what? They probably wanted to be together to watch your race."

"Dunno. I just thought it was strange. Anyway, what's up? Why have you…'called'?"

"I just wanted to say well done, Soph. When are you on next?"

"It's the last 32 on Sunday. I'm on about 6.30."

"I'll be looking out for you."

"Night-night, then Jack."

"Night, Soph. Soph?"

"Yes?"

"You did really well. I mean it. Well done."

He almost heard her sigh, "Night, Jack."

The first thing Jack noticed was the sound. The competitors' shoes squealed like cats fighting at night. The fencers moved so quickly. They danced forward and back. The points of their weapons zinged in the air with the speed of insects as they darted toward their opponents' bodies. A buzzer sounded. A light flashed red or green. The fencers stopped and their sword-points drooped. One of them had scored a hit.

It was happening so fast Jack couldn't see when the hit was made. He was sitting close to the action but it was still too fast for him to register. The fencers were like statues one second and then exploded into action. Thrust. Swerve. Flick. Thrust. The lights flashed and the fighters resumed their positions before flashing into a frenzy of movement once again. They carried on until a winner emerged.

When each bout finished, the fencers took off their masks and saluted each other. They were men and women of all ages and colours. They were dashing athletes who fought one on one. They moved too fast for the human eye. The judges needed technology to determine whether the sword point had made contact. Each fleeting duel only made sense when it was repeated in slow motion on the screens.

Jack's eyes never left the arena. When a new pair of competitors came to their marks, connected up their wires and went into the 'on-guard' position, his blood quickened. He dared not blink for missing the action.

The sport sparked a yearning deep inside him. He was stirred by the way the competitors fought anonymously, hidden by their masks. He loved the way fencers strutted about straight-backed like ballet dancers. The muscles on their calves cracked with power where they showed beneath the buttoned cuffs of their breeches.

When they announced the session was over for the day Jack was surprised to see three hours had passed.

"You there, Soph?"

"I'm in bed, Jack. I was nearly asleep. What's up?"

"Just wanted to think-talk."

"Think-talk?"

"What we're doing. It's got to have a name so I'm calling it think-talk."

Sophie's think-talk sigh came over loud and clear. "OK. Call it what you like. But let's get this over with. I need to get some sleep."

Jack was bursting to tell her about his enthusiasm for the sport he had discovered. "I just wanted to wish you all the best for tomorrow, Soph."

"Thanks, Jack. That's sweet. That all?"

"Yes."

"Good night, then."

"Good night."

On the next day, Sunday, Jack passed through the security for the fencing arena fizzing with anticipation. The previous day he had been trembling with trepidation. He had worried whether his competitors' security pass would take him through into the free seats reserved for athletes. Today he had no worries on that score but, if anything, his nerves were jangling more.

He took one of the seats amongst five or six other athletes. The first two competitors came onto the floor and took up their marks. Jack saw their swords were different. They had blades. The competitors put on their masks and stood opposite each other; on guard. The skirmish began. This time the moves were more savage. They weren't dancers, they were fighters, leaping toward each other, slashing. The swords clashed with the sound of knives being sharpened. Then the buzzer went and a light came on and they stepped back to their marks.

By the end of the second day's session, Jack was breathless with excitement. Audak hadn't told him why he had chosen fencing and it didn't matter. Jack had discovered a sport he wanted to do.

Later in the day, Sophie's face filled the screen. "Here she is, Sophie Donovan. The nation has certainly taken this young swimmer to its heart." The woman who was leading the discussion turned to one of the people in the studio with her. "What are her chances today, Sharron?"

"Sophie did really well to get here. She has a slightly better draw than before but she still has four competitors here who have better PBs than her. If they all swim to form, I'm afraid she's not going to make it."

The woman smiled, "But she beat the odds in her heat, Sharron. Let's see if she can do it again. Let's go poolside."

Jack was sitting in his room. He had a take-away pizza on his lap. The commentator's voice boomed out.

"Yes, here we are. The second quarter final. We saw Stella Lowe, another Briton, fail in the first heat so let's see if Sophie Donovan can go one stage better. They are on their marks."

The screen went silent. Jack's mouth gaped open. It was waiting to take in the slice of pie he held inches away but it didn't get any closer.

"Crack!" The sound of the starter's pistol was followed by the screams of the fans crowded into the stadium.

"Donovan has a reasonable start in lane three. She's into her stroke and is on the shoulder of the Russian, Yakutsov, in lane two. She's fourth but there's nothing between the first six as they come to the turn."

The pizza hovered in front of Jack's face.

"Donovan turns in fourth place. It's a qualifying position at this stage. The first four are pulling away. It looks like Donovan's going to be there in the semis."

"Go, Sophie," shouted Jack.

"Twenty-five metres to go. The Australian, Barnard, is putting in a spurt in lane one. She's moved up into fifth place and she's making ground on Donovan. Barnard is definitely a danger. I don't think Donovan has seen her. Donovan isn't breathing to that side. She doesn't know she's there. The crowd is screaming at her to speed up. She needs to finish strongly to keep her qualifying place."

"Sophie. Sophie." Jack could feel his sister switch on. He had the sensation of damp coolness around his skin. "The girl in lane one. She's catching you. Speed up if you can."

"No!" The single word filled his head as if Sophie had shouted it into his ear.

"No!" This time it was the commentator's voice from the screen. "Donovan's pulled up! Her stroke has gone. Barnard from Australia cruises past her. The Japanese swimmer Takato passes her. She's trailing in sixth. It's a tragedy for Donovan. She was so close."

"It was cheating, Jack." Sophie was think-talking later in the evening.

"But she was on your blindside. I was only telling you she was there."

"That's the whole point. If I was too stupid not to keep an eye on both sides, I deserved to lose."

"But I wanted you to qualify."

"Don't you think I wanted it too? Desperately."

"Well then—"

Sophie interrupted him, "You don't understand, do you, Jack? Of course I wanted it. But I wasn't going to do it like that."

There was a vacuum in both their heads in the space where they had got used to hearing each other's voices. It was Jack who filled it first. "Did they believe what you said?" He sensed his sister's confusion. "I saw the interview. You said you had cramp in the last few metres. Did they believe you?"

"Yeah. Well I couldn't say I stopped because my brother was cheating, could I? "

Jack smiled and wondered whether Sophie could sense he was amused. "No I suppose you couldn't. Look, I'm sorry Soph. I didn't mean to ruin your chances of getting in the semis."

"You didn't, Jack. I was going as fast as I could anyway. I've seen the replay. Barnard would have caught me. I was always out of it." Jack sensed her mood change, "But, I've still got the relay." There was a pause. "It's your big day tomorrow, Jack."

Jack knew she was thinking about the delivery of the computer. "Let's hope it arrives this time," he sent. "I just want to get on with the game and get out of here. It's been good to have you to talk to though, Sis."

"That man you're in touch with, the alien. Do you think he'll take away this thing we can do."

"Think-talk?" asked Jack.

"Yes."

"I'm not sure. We won't need it after this business with Zavorus is cleared up, will we? I suppose it means he will. It's been good, though, hasn't it? Night night, Soph."

"Night, Jack. And thanks for trying to help."

Amnugen in London

The computer arrived shortly after Jack returned from breakfast. Steve, the concierge, called ahead. Jack was holding the door open ready when the young delivery woman emerged from the lift lobby. She was pushing a trolley containing the box.

"Wow!" she said. "This is my first set-up in Olympic Park." She looked Jack up and down. "You must be really important if the standard machine's not good enough for you." Her dark-brown eyes were bright with excitement. "What do you do…?" She looked at the paper in her hand. "…Mr Gould."

Jack stepped forward and shook her hand, "Call me Brad." He returned to Audak's story. "I'm a fitness coach with the American squad. I need a good machine to download stuff from the States."

"But you're English," she said. "What are you doing helping the opposition?"

Jack had thought about the questions she might ask. "I've lived in the States for seven years. But you never lose your accent."

"Forgive me for saying so, but you don't look any older than me. I'm not giving anything away, but this is my first job and I haven't been doing it long. How come they give you a job like that?"

"I guess it's because of what I studied at college. Will it take long to set up?"

"What?" She waved a hand at the box. "This stuff. It's a doddle. I'll have you up and running…" She giggled. "Excuse the pun. Up and running in no time."

She smiled at Jack and locked his eyes with hers. "My name's Leanne, by the way."

Jack couldn't understand why he was blushing. "Nice to meet you, Leanne."

She stood still, looking at him with her head cocked to one side. A slab of black hair hung over her eye. "Yeah, well Brad, it's nice to meet you too."

She shook her head slightly as if to shake a fly off her nose. "I'd best be getting on."

Jack watched as Leanne removed the parts of the SN computer from its box and set them up together. He noticed how the permatint on her eyelids showed off the brown of her eyes. She handled the machinery expertly. It wasn't long before Leanne had the combi, computer and screen linked up and she was showing him through a list of popular websites.

"What's your domain name, Brad? I'll set it up as your start page if you like."

Jack had been mesmerised watching Leanne's flashing fingers as she had worked through the set-up programs. Her pink-painted nails intrigued him.

"Pardon?"

"Your domain page? I'll make it the start page."

"There's no need," he said. He tried to imagine what Leanne would look like in the evening if she was going out on a date. She wouldn't wear the brown nylon smock-top and trousers of her uniform, that was for sure.

"OK. I'll just put in your ident chip and then it'll be set up," she said.

"Huh?" Jack didn't want her to leave so soon.

"I've set it up with a test ident. I'll put your chip in and you'll be ready to rock 'n' roll."

Jack felt his colour rising again. "No, don't worry about the chip. I'll put it in." He thought as soon as Brad Gould's ident sent out its web signature, Audak's strange face would appear on the screen. It would freak Leanne out.

"Well, that's me all done, then." She smiled and cocked her head to one side again. "I'll just take all this packaging away." She seemed to be waiting for something.

"I'll give you a hand." Jack moved forward and picked up the discarded wrapping. He turned to put it in the box and his arm brushed against Leanne. It made him feel flustered. He put the plastic wrapping in the box she held open for him.

"Look," she said. "I should really set you up on your domain before I leave. Are you sure you're okay?"

"Yes," said Jack. "I know my way around SN technology."

"OK. Well, at least let me leave you on the Olympic Park home page. She pressed a few buttons on the combi and the Olympic page came up. The headline wiped Jack's mind clean as if it had been hit by a pandem.

Amnugen Corporation sponsors Olympic Park competitors' village, it read.

"Look, I'm sorry to be rude, Leanne, but I've got to get on. The new computer was ordered last week originally. I've got a lot of catching up to do."

Leanne looked disappointed. "I was hoping you might buy me a coffee so as I could have a better look around while I was here."

Jack spread his hands wide. "It's a nice idea, Leanne. But I really do have to get on." He pushed the trolley out of the room and ushered her out behind it. "Sorry, but I really have got loads of work to do."

As soon as he was alone, Jack read the rest of the story: *International global energy conglomerate Amnugen Corporation of Grand Rapids, Michigan has announced a late Olympic sponsorship deal. It has become the official sponsor of the Olympic Village. This is a direct result of the acquisition of the Sustainable Energy Release from Super-Ice (SERSI) technology programme. The company is expected to expand quickly and the management views the Olympic Village as a potential international training centre. A spokesperson said, "Amnugen has taken a preliminary look at the competitors' village. The sponsorship of the village gives us first option to buy the site once the Games are over and Olympic Park becomes a prime commercial and residential feature of London's future. From today, the Olympic Village is now called the Amnugen Olympic Village."*

Jack wasn't interested in the rest of the article. He had to talk to Audak fast. He put the Brad Gould ident chip in the combi and refreshed the web set-up. The screen went green. It was blank except for the two icons of Audak's face. Jack had been right not to let Leanne see this. He tagged the communication icon.

The chat box appeared, *Connecting...*

Audak's text followed: *Hello, Brad. Can we talk?*

Jack's fingers flew over the text buttons: *Yes. Have you seen what Amnugen has done? What does this mean?*

Zavorus must have picked up your web signature when you started the game by mistake. He has tracked you down. The Olympic Park security is the best there is. He is using this sponsorship to get access to you.

Jack tagged 'yes' to allow visual contact and Audak's kindly face appeared.

"But it's costing them millions," protested Jack.

"Remember Zavorus has influence over what the people around him are thinking. They believe they are doing the sponsorship because the site will make a good training centre." Jack was still not used to Audak's lips not moving and hearing the synthetic voice.

"Does it mean he's coming here?"

"Yes. It probably does."

"Does he intend to harm me?"

"We think it's not likely. If he gets close to you, he can influence you. If he's near you when you are sleeping, it's possible for him to make you forget all about the game and why you are there. You must move ahead with the game as quickly as possible."

"It's going to take at least two days. It won't take him long to find me."

"We are trying to think of an alternative plan. Start the game. We will see what happens. Remember you have your sibling. I assume you have discovered our little surprise." His eyes crinkled around the edges.

"How did you do that?"

"It is a part of your brain your species no longer uses. We just had to spark it to life while you were both asleep. It is only possible because you are brother and sister. It would have been even easier if you were genetically the same."

"Identical twins, you mean."

"Yes. Identical. Did it help you, Jack?"

"Yes. It was good to have somebody to tell. But it was difficult for her to accept that we could do this think-talk."

"It will become second nature to you. It is with us."

"Then I had to tell her about you and Zavorus. It wasn't easy."

"We prepared her brain while she was asleep. She was more receptive than if we had done nothing."

"I wouldn't like to have tried without your help, then." Jack saw the creasing around Audak's eyes.

"You can use your sister's help to stay ahead of Zavorus. We have to assume he will come to the Olympic Park. We are working on the assumption for the alternative plan."

Jack looked at his watch as soon as the screen went blank. Sophie's morning training would be over. He think-talked her name, "Sophie!"

He received a lot of confused messages back. He couldn't make sense of it.

"Sophie!"

"Jack. You can't appear out of the blue like that. I was having coffee with some team-mates. It's not easy to be in a conversation and think-talk at the same time."

"Where are you now?"

"In the food centre. The coffee shop."

"Can we meet over there. Can you lose your friends? It's urgent. I've been talking to Audak. We need to start working together on the game thing."

Workmen were hanging a new banner over the entrance to the food centre. Jack waited until he was able to read it. *Welcome to Amnugen Olympic Village*, it said. Despite the sun on his back, Jack felt cold. He ducked under the banner and went inside the food centre.

Sophie was sitting alone in one of the leather armchairs. Jack thought she looked more grown up than he had seen before. There was an awkward moment before they hugged briefly. Jack noticed his sister watching him while he ordered his coffee and returned to the table.

"You look different, Jack. More grown up."

"I was going to say the same about you, Soph. My excuse is I'm seventeen – according to my security tags." He held them up for her to see. "What's yours?"

"It's this whole thing." She waved her arms around her. "Being part of the team. They don't treat me like the baby. They make me believe I'm the equal of anybody here. I suppose it makes you think you're older. Anyway, what's the latest on your adventure?"

"Did you see about the Amnugen Corporation sponsorship? It was on the Web this morning."

"No, I've been chilling this morning. I'm doing light training only until the relays. What sponsorship?"

"Didn't you see the banners? They, Amnugen Corporation, are sponsoring the Competitors' Village. It's supposedly so they get first option to buy it after the games are over. But Audak thinks it's so Zavorus can get into the village. He knows I'm here."

Sophie put her glass down on the table so sharply she splashed some of the juice. "That's it, Jack. You have to go to the police, the security people, whatever. You can't put yourself in danger for this totally mad thing you've got into. What if it's some kind of hoax?"

"Audak says I'm not in danger. Not of violence. Zavorus will try and stop me completing the game using his mind-power."

Sophie snorted, "Don't you see how ridiculous this sounds, Jack? Aliens with mind-power?"

Jack could feel the blood rushing to his head and tears started burning his eyes. "Don't you think I've tried to work all this out with rational explanations? Things that don't involve aliens and stuff. What about the think-talking thing? Audak told me I'd be able to get your help. Next thing we know is we've got this telepathy going on between us." He rubbed his eyes. "What about all the computer hacking that was needed to get me in here. It has to be down to an intelligence bigger than ours."

Sophie placed her hands flat on the table and slowed her breathing down. "So let's agree it is aliens, Jack." She looked around. Anybody who heard them talking calmly about aliens like this would think they were crazy. "Don't you think somebody – the authorities – ought to know what's going on?"

Jack voice was low. "I've thought about that as well. But what would happen? They'd think I was mad. They'd lock me up. They'd say I was a criminal for getting in here. They'd treat me like a terrorist. I wouldn't be able to finish the game. Audak wouldn't be able to get Zavorus back. He'd be able carry on with his plan to steal our water."

"When you talk like that, Jack, it sounds even crazier!"

"I know. The problem is, it's the truth. I didn't choose it. It chose me. I have to see it through."

Sophie let go one of her big sighs. "So you really think it's the only thing you can do?"

Jack looked her in the eyes. "Yes. And if Zavorus is on his way here, I'm going to need you to watch out for me while I play the game."

Jack was hunched over the counter at the combi-point in the food centre. It was his second session of the day. He had played solidly for three hours after the meeting with Sophie. He was lost in the Zombietown scenery. He zapped the zombies and was sure he would soon get sight of the face at the window. He assumed, this time, it would be Audak's.

Occasionally, he looked up from where he sat to make sure Sophie was watching from her position on the floor above. She could see anybody approach him. She think-talked to him from time to time to let him know how bored she was. All he could do was remind her he was in danger without her help.

During the break, while Sophie went for a training session, Jack took some time off in the fencing arena. He chose one competitor in each bout and studied their moves. He could see when they made the decision to move from defence into attack. His mind whirred with the flashing blades. He was still not quick enough to see the point of contact, when the tip of the foil or epee found its target, but was able to predict whose light would flash first to signal a hit.

He loved the combination of dance and wristwork needed for the finer disciplines but was put off by the raw violence of the sabre. When he took up fencing he was going to be an artist, not a savage.

Sophie think-talked she was ready to resume her vigil and they met by a different combi-point. Jack tagged the game icon and Sophie took her station on a seat in the floor above. She watched the people, predominately athletes, as they passed by without taking any notice of the young man in a track-suit amusing himself with a computer game.

While he played, Jack's mind worked on two levels. He was playing by instinct. The conscious part of his mind was trying to work out how his actions were creating a program on his computer that would bring Audak to earth. He decided the brickwork of the buildings held the key. He had always thought the structures were unnecessarily detailed. Now he realised, as his figure moved, his shadow passed over the walls. He noticed, when it was touched, a brick would shimmer for a moment before resuming its previous state.

Jack became increasingly convinced each brick represented a segment of code. Zavorus had created the game so Jack's shadow had to follow a prescribed route. When Jack went out of sequence, he was shot from behind. Thus Zavorus made Jack's shadow pass over the bricks in his pre-determined order. By playing the game, Jack was putting the code into its proper sequence. The nearer Jack was to the end of the game, the closer it was to being a fully-fledged program. In the final scene, when Jack zapped Audak, the program would be initiated and Audak would be transported to Earth.

His attention was broken by Sophie. "Jack, I'm tired of this. Can we stop now?"

He thought for a second she was standing beside him. Then he remembered think-talk. "Yeah, you're right. It's getting late." A hotel appeared at the next corner. He turned into the lobby. Audak was still there. He hadn't started appearing at windows but Jack reckoned he would soon. He thought he was about a third of the way through the game.

"D'you fancy some supper?" Jack asked.

"Yes. Let's go to the fish place. I've been there. It's really good."

Jack groaned, "Fish? Do we have to?" Then he thought about the evenings he had eaten alone. "Actually, Soph. Fish is fine. Great. Come down. Let's go."

Zavorus

We are monitoring the game. You are doing well. How long do you think you need? Audak asked in the chat box.

I think I'm about a third of the way through: Jack texted back.

Yes. It is what we calculate. If you can start earlier and get some uninterrupted time you can finish tomorrow.

Jack tagged the vision icon and spoke, "Yeah. I don't get so tired like last time. I hardly ever have to go back because I've done something wrong. So I'm speeding up as well. I'll be glad when it's finished."

"Yes. So shall we. You have done well, Jack."

Jack nodded, "What will you do to take Zavorus back?"

"I merely have to be in the same dimension as him, Jack. It is difficult for you to understand. He will know when I am there and his behaviour will change. It is very difficult to be a renegade in our species because our minds are all connected closely, even more closely than you and Sophie. He will not be able to operate. I will be a focus for the collective power of all our people. It will be against him. He will not have a choice. He will have to return."

"What about the energy plant he's building?"

"We will take care of it."

"So, one more day then."

"Yes. We hope, one more day. Good luck, Jack."

Next morning, Jack think-talked Sophie first thing and was rewarded with the cool, damp feeling on his skin. "Sorry, I can feel you're swimming, Soph," he sent.

"Later!"

Sophie's voice appeared in his head an hour later. "Have you had breakfast?" she asked.

"Not yet."

"What about it? I need to have something."

"Yes. Can we meet somewhere else today? I ought to use a different combi-point for each session."

"OK."

Once they were together, Jack took his juice and croissants to the combi point and started up the game. Sophie watched from the breakfast counter.

"Everything OK?" he think-talked.

"Looking good," she answered.

As Jack had suspected, it didn't take long for Audak to appear at a window. Jack was speeding up taking out the zombies in quick succession. Soon the good guys in blue would arrive to help him and he'd go even faster. He calculated it would all be over by the middle of the afternoon.

"Jack, Jack!" It was Sophie.

Jack jerked himself back to reality. "What is it?" he asked.

"A man. He's walking funny. Sort of not using his knees properly. He's sliding his feet forward. Amongst all these athletes. It's so out of place."

"Where is here?"

"Over by the gift shop. You know, the tacky souvenirs."

Jack pressed the pause button and risked a quick look over his shoulder. A man in a light blue suit had his back to the combi-point. He was wearing a dark baseball cap and was looking down.

"What's he looking at?" Jack asked.

"His combi. He's moving it around. Have you still got the game on?"

"Yes."

"Quickly! Close it down. I don't like the look of him."

Jack looked at the screen. A hotel sign had appeared during the pause. He restarted the game and headed for the sign.

"What are you doing, Jack? The man's spun round. He's pointing his combi straight at you. Quick, get out of there!"

Jack rushed into the hotel and the screen went dead. He picked up his combi and started walking towards the nearest exit. "What's happening?" he asked.

"He's seen you leave. He's by where you were sitting. He's looking round. Oh! He's spotted me."

"Look away. Don't look like you've been watching him."

"I'm not."

Jack was out in the open. He went through one of the exits into the park and walked briskly toward his favourite arena. He was soon among the public streaming in for the afternoon's events.

"Sophie, what's happening now?"

"I've not been looking at him, have I?" Jack detected panic in her thoughts. "He's still there. He's looking at me again. I can see something on his cap. Oh no! It's the Amnugen logo, Jack. I think it's him. I think it's Zavorus."

They arranged to meet at one of the public coffee places in Olympic Park. It was nicely crowded.

"I'm so close to finishing the game, Sophie. I've got to carry on." Jack banged his fist on the table.

Sophie's eyes were staring and her voice had a higher tone than usual. "I think Zavorus knows I'm looking out for you."

"Yeah. I don't think you being there will help." He was thinking frantically. "His combi must be able to detect the web signal. He's going to track me down every time I start the game up."

"And if Audak's right, he can stop you from finishing using his mind power."

"Do you think here's here legitimately?" asked Jack, even though he knew the answer.

"Yeah. The cap's a giveaway isn't it? He's here because of the sponsorship."

130

"I know what I'm going to do." His knuckles were pale as he gripped his cup. "I'm going to stay out here in the public area until I finish. I'll move around all the combi-points so he won't know where I'm going to be next. Thank goodness he can't move fast."

"What should I do? I can still be your look-out."

"He knows what you're doing so if we split up it'll make it harder for him to find me. Anyway, you'll be safer back at your place. He's only interested in stopping the game."

Jack's face was dark with determination. His brow was low over his eyes. "If I can stay one step ahead of him for an hour or so, I'm going to make it."

Thirty minutes later Jack was at his third combi-point. He'd reckoned he should spend a maximum of eight minutes at each location. He had criss-crossed the public area of Olympic Park using two outside combi-points and now he was inside the hall where the boxing was taking place. It wouldn't take much longer.

"How's it going, Jack?" It was Sophie.

He continued the game while he think-talked. "It's going OK. I'm in the boxing hall. I'm hoping Zavorus won't have access to competitors' areas. It should give me an advantage. Maybe I can stay here a bit longer."

"Well. Good luck. I'm just leaving the room. I can't stay here. I'm going for a swim. I need to stretch."

"All right, Sis. Look after yourself."

A few minutes later, Jack was hurrying to the next combi point, when Sophie interrupted his thoughts. "Jack! Jack! It's him. He's here! He's at the training pool."

Jack stopped and was jostled by passers-by, who looked at him strangely. "Sophie! Who? Sophie!" As his brain emptied of Sophie's thoughts, Jack knew who Sophie had seen. It was Zavorus. He cursed and started running toward the Aquatic Centre.

His combi alert sounded. He knew it was a problem. Only Sophie had Brad Gould's number. He pressed the 'call' button.

"Hello, Jack. It's Sophie. Are you OK?"

"Yes." His mind was racing. What did this mean?

"Would you like to come over? To my apartment?"

She must have known he would search the pools and go to her room next. Why did she bother to call?

He tried to stay calm while he figured things out. "What's up?"

"I've got somebody here. He says he wants to meet you. His name is Professor Zavorus."

Jack calculated how long he needed to finish the game. "I'll be there in twenty minutes." It would be tight.

Jack heard a wheezing, hissing with menace. Then a synthesized voice broke in. "You come straight away, Jack, unless you want your sister's brain turned to mush. After I've finished with her, a one-year-old baby would be able to swim faster." The impersonal sing-song of his voice made Jack's skin crawl. He swore under his breath.

The line went dead. Jack clung to one glimmer of hope. Zavorus had some sort of influence over Sophie's brain; that was obvious. But he didn't seem to know about their telepathy. If he had, he wouldn't have made Sophie use the combi.

He stopped at the nearest combi-point. "Come on, come on," he spoke aloud after tagging Audak's icon. He was wringing his hands unaware of the attention he was attracting from passers by.

Jack zapped in text as soon as the chat box appeared: *Zavorus has kidnapped Sophie. I have to meet him or he'll harm her. I only have minutes to get there.*

Audak's response was immediate: *We must go to our back-up plan. It can only work if you and Zavorus are together. We will take over all the screens in Olympic Park in five Earth minutes. We will put the transportation icon on the screens. You must tag the icon with your combi. But you must be holding on to Zavorus when you do it. If you do not have hold of him, it will not work. It is the only chance. Do you understand?*

Jack hit the keys frantically: *Screen shows icon. Tag on icon. But have to be holding on to Zavorus. OK?*

Again, Audak's answer came almost before he'd finished: *Yes. Good luck.*

Jack hesitated and hit the text keys again: *If we could do this all along, why wasn't this the first plan?*

Jack could sense the impatience in Audak's response: *We didn't know Zavorus would ever risk being in the same room as you. It shows how dangerous you are to his plans. We can control the transportation program from here if you can initiate it at your end. Now you have to hurry, Jack. Make sure you are actually touching him when you tag the icon.*

Jack didn't bother to respond. He ran off toward the British team building.

Jack didn't know what to expect when he walked up to the concierge's desk. His name must have appeared on the security screen. The concierge greeted him, "Mr Gould? You can go straight up. Ms Donovan's expecting you. Room 315."

He knocked on the door. The face of the man who opened it was not horribly disfigured as he had seen in the pictures. It was strangely pink and smooth.

"Come in, Jack. I see you are surprised." The man's lips didn't move and the synthesized voice came out of a speaker at his throat. He pointed at his face with gloved hands. "Do you like my disguise? Come in."

He stood aside to let Jack into the room. "Let me help you with that," he said, taking the combi from Jack's hand. Jack's self-belief drained away; he had allowed Zavorus to take his only weapon.

His heart lurched even lower when he saw Sophie sitting in the easy chair. She was looking at the screen with unblinking eyes.

"Your sister seems to have developed a keen interest in archery," Zavorus sneered. "We will let her stay there, I think."

Jack turned to face him. "You'll never get away with it." The words sounded hollow. "Audak will find a way to get here." He wished his voice was more self-assured.

Zavorus hissed behind the mask. "So you call my brother Audak? How quaint. It means 'the good one'." He wheezed while the synthesiser spoke for him. "You do not know how long it took me to find you, Jack. I had to wait for your species to develop the SN technology. You're a very slow race. Ha! I think I have made a joke. Slow race. It's very good in Olympic time." He shook his head. "It will take Audak, as you call him, many years to find another way of getting here. By that time I will have completed the plant in America. I will already be super-freezing ice and sending it back to Consobrina. His power will be gone."

"But, we'll find out the process is losing water; that you're stealing it from us," protested Jack. "Our scientists will see the water levels are going down in the lakes where you have your plants. We will stop you and Amnugen."

Zavorus shook his head. "By the time you Earth-people wake up to what is happening, you will be hooked on the cheap energy my process provides. Nobody will stop us. Did anybody care about killing your planet with global warming? I don't think so. What makes you think it will be different this time? If we hadn't taken your excess carbon emissions away, your planet would be dying now. I'm just shortening the borrowed time my people have given you."

Jack slumped on the bed and Zavorus moved slowly round the room so he was standing next to Sophie. He put the combi down on the shelf beneath the screen, which was silently showing an archer releasing his arrows. "As you can see, your sister is under my control. Now it's your turn."

"What have you done to her?"

"Don't worry. It's a straightforward hypnosis. She will wake up when I let her and all will be well – for her. With you, it's going to be more difficult. You have to forget everything. For that I think..." He undid his shirt collar and started picking at his neck. Slowly a flap of loose skin emerged and he tugged at it. He was pulling a layer of skin away to reveal the same dry surface Jack had seen on Audak. Zavorus's gloved fingers struggled to grip the thin membrane. It slowly peeled away from his chin. A lipless mouth was revealed. The flat nose appeared next. Finally, the whole of Zavorus's reptile-like face was exposed. Jack could imagine a forked tongue slithering between those lips. But all that came out of the dark hole was rasping breath.

Zavorus's other, human face was now hinged at the eyebrows and rested on top of his head like a grotesque cap. "I need to see your eyes, Jack," he said.

Jack knew instinctively it was the last thing he should do.

"That's it, just let me see your eyes."

Jack was able to resist the sing-song of the synthesizer. It was a sinister, more insistent voice inside his head he was struggling against. It made Jack turn toward Zavorus.

At that moment the screen flickered and broke up. It changed to plain green with a single icon shaped like an arrow. The second Jack took in the change, he launched himself at Zavorus. Jack's shoulder hit him at chest level and they crashed into the wall beneath the screen. Jack had estimated Zavorus would weigh much more. The force of his charge had taken him past his target and he had to reach back and up to the shelf for the combi. He grabbed it. The movement made him relax his hold on Zavorus, who squirmed away.

"I see. Audak has a new plan for me." The voice was unaffected by their struggle but Zavorus was wheezing even more loudly. "If you try it again, Jack, I'll have to wipe your brain clean. You'll be just like one of the zombies in the game you played so well for me"

Jack was also gasping for breath. Zavorus's threat made him feel stupid and angry for getting involved. In his fury he lunged at Zavorus with the combi. He missed. How he wished it was a fencing weapon.

"Relax, Jack. Relax."

Jack could feel his muscles loosen. He tried to focus on the screen. He knew Audak could not control the computers for long. He had only seconds left before the logo disappeared. He had one last chance. Zavorus didn't know about think-talk. "Sophie!" There was no reaction. "Sophie! Wake up."

Zavorus turned his head like dog hearing a silent whistle. The synthesizer squawked and went silent. A new voice, the wheezing, rasping sound of an alien, burst inside Jack's head. "What is that? What are you doing, Jack?"

Jack tried to ignore him. He focused entirely on his link to Sophie, "Help me, Soph! I've got to get hold of him." Jack sensed Zavorus had taken a step forward and was now standing between him and Sophie. He heard the hissing speech in his head, "What's this. Can you...? You're finished, Jack..."

Jack's head was suddenly filled with a shrieking sound as if all the banshees in the netherworld had risen up and screamed into his ears at the same time. He put his hands to his head, conscious his grip on the combi was loosening. But covering his ears was pointless. Zavorus had stirred up an electrical storm in his head so his brain was literally short-circuiting. Every cell was like a fuse that would burn out leaving him eternally senseless.

Jack opened his eyes as his knees gave way. Peering out from behind his pain-narrowed eyelids, Jack could see Zavorus's face radiating triumph.

The screaming in Jack's head abated for a second so Zavorus could sneer his victory. "It's a pity you won't be able to tell Audak you failed him, Jack. Do not be concerned, though, I will be happy to tell him for you once I have taken control of Consobrina…"

Jack was only dimly aware the convulsions in his head had reduced. He ignored Zavorus's voice. He only knew this was his last chance. He threw the last vestiges of his mental energy into thrusting his thoughts into his sister's unresponsive mind. "Help me, Sophie. You're acting like a pod person. For God's sake snap out of it!" A picture of their mother flooded his mind with calm as he sensed Sophie react.

She growled like a tiger disturbed. The noise turned into a full-throated roar. Zavorus turned to the sound. Sophie rose out her chair and flung herself at him. Jack, who had collapsed to his knees, tightened his grip on the combi at the moment Sophie made contact. She drove Zavorus backward into Jack's arms. He grabbed hold tightly so Zavorus was sandwiched between the twins. Jack raised the combi and pointed it at the icon. He tagged it first time and collapsed.

The bundle of soft-edged bones between them flashed with heat for an instant and was gone. Only the pale-blue suit and the cap with the Amnugen logo remained. Sophie was looking down at her hand. She was holding Zavorus's pinkly-limp rubbery face and sandy hairpiece.

The screen flashed. The Victorian pavilion of Lord's cricket ground resumed its place behind a row of targets. The archery was back on screen.

Closing Ceremony

They passed the concierge's desk at the entrance to the residents' lounge.

"Excuse me, Miss?"

They stopped. They were carrying Zavorus's clothes, mask and security tags in a carrier bag.

"What happened to your other guest, Miss? Guests have to be accompanied at all times."

Sophie looked surprised. "He left a while ago. While there was a problem with the screens. Perhaps it wasn't picked up. Were the computers down?"

"Nice one, Sis," Jack think-talked. A lingering headache appeared to be the only effect of his encounter with Zavorus.

The young man looked puzzled. "Well, it's not logged on the system. I'll look into it."

"I need to sort this out, Soph. You go and order me a smoothie and I'll be with you soon."

He stopped at the nearest combi-point. When Brad's domain appeared he clicked on the communication icon. He texted as soon as the connection was made: *Is he back?*

Yes. We have him: wrote Audak.

So it's all under control?

Yes.

Jack tagged the icon for visual contact. "I still don't see why you couldn't have got him back that way before," said Jack.

"I will try to explain," said Audak. "The transportation program has to be initiated at the receiving end. It is why Zavorus made you play the game to create and initiate the program at your end. But it still needs cooperation at the sending end. There was no chance of tricking Zavorus into sending himself so our first plan was for me to follow him and take him back. We needed you to play the game again to take me there."

"I get it," said Jack. "It was only possible to go to the second plan once you knew Zavorus and I would be in the room together."

"Exactly," answered Audak in the same synthesiser voice that sounded so chilling when Zavorus was using it. "We were running the program at the receiving end but we needed your cooperation to tag the icon when the coordinates were all lined up. It is why you had to have him in your grip. We transported all Consobrinan matter within an area around your combi."

"That's how Sophie and I got left behind."

"And his earth clothes," said Audak, his eyes doing the crinkling thing.

Jack put his hand to his head. "When Zavorus realised we could think-talk he tried to fry my brain. My head was full of noise. I thought I was going to die."

"You must have been very brave to resist it. Don't worry. If the burn-out process didn't reach its conclusion there are no lasting effects. Although, your head will have a pain for some days."

Jack nodded. "We have a few loose ends here. We have to explain Zavorus's disappearance," he said.

"We have looked at the security records for Amnugen personnel. Zavorus came to Britain pretending to be an Amnugen employee called Patrick Santorini. Zavorus created this identity so he could get into the village. His story was that he was doing a survey for when Amnugen buys it. Santorini doesn't really exist. It will be easy to change the security records of the Olympic Village to show he has left the building and the park. You will not have problems."

"Good. What about the energy plant?"

"It is already dealt with, Jack."

"That's it then."

"Yes, Jack. You did well. It is not possible to estimate the benefit of what you have done. You have saved your planet."

Jack fought to keep his face cool. "But I won't be able to tell anybody, will I?"

Audak's eyes crinkled. "I'm afraid not. Nobody will believe you. Once we finish this link, all records on your computer will be destroyed."

"But what about what happened to all the computers in the Olympic Village?"

"We have already made sure there are explanations for everything."

"So, it's goodbye then."

"Goodbye, Jack, and thank you."

"Can you do me one favour, Audak?"

"What is it, Jack?"

"Can I keep the Brad Gould identity until the games are over?

"Of course, Jack. Farewell."

"You know I'm going to work out how to get through to your dimension, don't you? I will do it."

But there was no answer. Audak had already closed the link.

A banana and peach smoothie was waiting on the table when Jack got back. As he sat down, he spotted athletes in the room who he'd seen on screen.

Sophie noticed his eyes widening. "What's the matter. Haven't you got used to this yet?" she asked.

"I've not seen so many famous faces in one room before."

"There must be many more famous ones in the American building."

"I've never dared to go to the residents' lounge. They might have asked me what I was doing."

The volume of the nearest screen increased and they recognised the music introducing the news.

"Welcome to the six o'clock news on a day which has seen extraordinary activity from the centre of our solar system. Unprecedented levels of nuclear energy release, called sunspots, have caused massive disruption to computers around the world. In London, some events in the Olympic Games were interrupted as all the computer screens went blank. We are going over to Olympic Park…"

The twins smiled at each other. "Sunspots," said Jack. "Audak said there would be an explanation."

"Are you going to tell me what happened to Zavorus?"

"Audak explained it. They were always able to transport him back, if they could pinpoint exactly where he was at a particular time and had somebody at this end to initiate the program. When they knew Zavorus and I were going to meet, they arranged for the send part of the program to be ready on all the screens in Olympic Park. I had to hold on to him and tag the icon to initiate the system. He was really hurting my head. Thanks to you, I was able to get hold of him. He's gone back to Consobrina."

"How come we didn't go as well?"

"The transporting system only recognised certain types of matter – stuff from Consobrina."

They looked up at the screen again. "…and in what is thought to be another effect of the solar activity there has been a massive explosion at the Amnugen research laboratory on the banks of Lake Michigan. This is the plant where a Professor Zavorus had invented a new process to generate renewable energy cheaply. We are able to talk to an Amnugen Corporation spokeswoman on the site." The newsreader turned to a screen in his studio. Jack and Sophie saw a woman with a microphone. She was wearing a baseball cap like the one Zavorus had worn earlier.

"Can you tell us what happened?"

"Yes. We experienced the same problems with our computers as affected some other locations like your Olympic Park. This caused a small fire in one of our laboratories and the building was evacuated. The last person, or we thought the last person, had left the building when there was a massive explosion in Professor Zavorus's private laboratory. The fires spread to the rest of the plant and it's totally destroyed."

"Was Professor Zavorus there?"

"It's too early to be certain but, unfortunately, we believe he was. He hadn't been seen for 72 hours. It is not unusual for him. His own personal quarters were in that part of the building. He often stayed there, without contacting us, for as long as a week."

"He was the victim of a similar accident before, wasn't he?"

The woman shuffled uncomfortably. "Yes," she answered.

"Does this mean the process Professor Zavorus was working on is not safe?"

"That is speculation at this stage. What concerns us at the moment is Professor Zavorus's safety. The explosion was so severe it is unlikely any traces of his presence will be detectable. If that's the case we have to hope he will turn up."

"But will you continue his work?"

"Amnugen Corporation will try to pick up the pieces but this was Professor Zavorus's process. If he is dead it may die with him."

Jack turned to Sophie. "It's just as Audak said. There's nothing left to show what's happened."

"There is something," he heard Sophie say, before he realised her lips hadn't moved.

"There is that," he think-talked back.

The house didn't look any different. The curtains twitched in the house opposite. He steeled himself and walked up the garden path and rang the doorbell.

Mrs Donovan only had time to shout, "Jack! Jack!" before she burst into tears.

Later, they sat at the kitchen table, drinking tea. Mrs Donovan had composed herself and called her husband to tell him the news. He left work immediately.

"Why, Jack, why?" she asked for about the fifth time. This time she waited for an answer.

Sophie and he had worked something out. "It was what was happening with Sophie, Mum. It was getting too much."

Mrs Donovan nodded her head vigorously, splashing tears onto the table. "I knew it. I told Max a thousand times. It's hard for Jack, being her twin."

He had to explain everything again when his dad arrived.

"Where did you go, son?" he asked after he'd finished the longest and hardest hug Jack could remember.

"I just hung about in London, Dad."

"What did you do for money?"

"I had a bit put by."

Mrs Donovan ruffled his hair. "Let's not interrogate the boy, Max. He's home. He's safe. It's all that counts."

As the evening approached, an awkward silence seemed to fall over his parents. Jack didn't understand. Something was going on. Finally he asked, "What's up, Mum."

"We don't know what to do, Son."

"What about?"

"It's the relay final. It's on in five minutes." She looked concerned. "We understand if you'd rather not."

"I forgot all about it," said Jack. "I came home to watch it with you." He looked at his watch, "Come on, we're just in time."

The three of them turned to the screen, and Mr Donovan turned up the sound.

"...so you think our medal chances are not good, then." The studio presenter was talking to the commentator at the pool-side on a split screen.

"We only scraped through to the final. Realistically, I think we'll be swimming for fifth or sixth place."

"Well it looks like the teams are gathering by the pool, so over to you for the four by one-hundred freestyle women's final."

The pistol cracked and Jack could sense his mother and father tense. Sophie was swimming second. At the end of the first leg Britain was in fourth place.

"Now we have Britain's youngest-ever swimmer, Sophie Donovan. Sharron, she's going to do well to hold her own in this competition."

"Well she's certainly started fast. She's already making inroads into the third swimmer's lead."

"Yes, it's a superb swim. She's coming up to the turn in third place. This is a really good swim."

"I fear her inexperience may be showing here." Sharron said. "She's gone off too fast. She's well up on her personal best. The excitement has got to her. I think she's going to pay for this in the final twenty metres."

"Rubbish, she knows what she's doing!" shouted Mr Donovan.

"Halfway up the second leg and now she's in second place. If anything she's looking stronger, Sharron. She's fighting for the lead. Come on, Sophie! Come on!"

"Go, Sophie!" The Donovans were all on their feet willing Sophie to the finish.

"I'm not sure," said Sharron. "Frankly, I don't think she can keep this up."

Mrs Donovan shook her fist at the screen. "You're talking out of your backside, woman!" she shouted. "Go, Sophie! Go!"

"Ten metres to go and she's still going strong." The commentator was screeching, "Come on, Britain! Come on, Sophie!"

"Go on, Sophie!" The Donovans were waving and shouting. They watched as Sophie touched at the same time as the leader. The third British swimmer dived in.

"Thanks to the stupendous swim from Sophie Donovan we're in second place, Sharron. We're going to win a medal after all! Great swim, Sophie! Come on, Britain!"

"It was an amazing swim from Sophie Donovan. She knocked more than four seconds off her previous best. It's really brought us up. It's game on for Britain."

The rest of the commentary was lost as the Donovan family roared the rest of the team home. They couldn't hold on to second place but Sophie had won a medal – bronze.

"It'll be gold next time," said Mr Donovan as he whirled around the room.

Mrs Donovan was crying again. "Oh, Max, a bird in the hand. A bird in the hand. We're happy with bronze aren't we, Jack?"

Jack watched the team of four women hugging and jumping together as they celebrated their medal. He tried a short think-talk message. "Well done, Sis," he said. "Gold next time, eh?"

He saw her tilt her head and put her finger to her ear. She'd heard, even though the twins were over a hundred miles apart.

Jack ran away again ten days later. This time he left a note. It said he had some unfinished business in London and would be back next day.

Brad Gould arrived at the Olympic Village four hours later. His security passes worked without a hitch. He headed for the competitors' village and sat in front of a coffee shop which gave him good view of the British accommodation.

The athletes began to move off toward the arena in time for the relay finals. He saw Sophie and slid down behind the paper he was reading. He made sure his mind was clear of any think-talk.

He followed the athletes to the main stadium and slid in among them as they went through security. Brad Gould's competitor's pass allowed him to follow them in.

The music started and they moved off into the arena. Camera flashes sparkled like fireworks as they entered. Jack felt his hair swept back by the noise of the spectators roaring. He stood with thousands of other athletes as the final speeches were made. They watched as the Olympic flame was passed to representatives from Johannesburg.

The first of the fireworks burst high above them, red, white and blue. The music started and they moved off to parade, dancing around the track. Jack who had kept his eye on Sophie all along, crept up beside her and grabbed her waist.

"Jack! I thought you were at home." She had to shout to make herself heard.

"I couldn't miss this, could I?"

"It's great you came," she said and they hugged.

He broke away and spun around so the lights and sounds became a whirl in his brain. "Isn't this brilliant, Sis?" he shouted. "You did fabulously. Bronze medal winner. You're the greatest."

She was laughing and jumping up and down. The bronze medal around her neck was flying and catching the floodlights. "I am. I'm the greatest," she screamed. "But what about you, Jack? You saved the world."

It was Jack's turn to throw his arms out. "I saved the world!" he shouted. The celebrating athletes surrounding them didn't even notice.

"I'm going to join you, Soph." Jack grasped her arm to show he was serious as he shouted in her ear. "I'm going to do this. Do it properly. It may not be Johannesburg, but the one after. I'm going to take up fencing. I'm going to make the team."

"We'll both be there, Jack. A team within a team."

She pointed to some other athletes who held their combis up to send pictures home.

"Shall we?" she asked.

"Why not?"

Sophie screeched to make herself heard above the music and the excited chattering around them. "Hey Mum, Dad. Look at this!" She held the combi up so they could see her face against the backdrop of the stadium. She could hear the commentary in the living room of Mr Donovan's apartment.

Jack moved into view. They both heard their mother squeal, "Who's with you?"

He moved closer.

"It's Jack! Jack, what are you doing there?"

"Where there's a will there's a way, Mum."

They all laughed. Jack and Sophie watched as Mrs Donovan wiped tears from her eyes. Their father slipped an arm round their mother's waist and pulled her closer.